Driftwood

An anthology

Writers in Stone

Contents

Introduction

Stories inspired by a photograph

A Definition of Excitement	Fenja Hill	11
Uncle Pete	Elizabeth Lawrence	14
Bride and Groom	Elizabeth Lawrence	16
Ballet Rehearsal, 1873	Macaque	17

A story in 50 words

50 Words about Fear	Macaque	21
Just a Trim	Louise Pople	22
The Proposal	Elizabeth Lawrence	23
50 Words about Love	Macaque	24

The Bay

Lifelines	Elizabeth Lawrence	27
The Sunfold	Macaque	31
The Bay	Louise Pople	32

Euphonic Writing

This is the entrance…	Lois Elsden	37
Yin and Yang	Elizabeth Lawrence	39
The Bone-Yard	Macaque	41

Reflections

Mirror Images	Elizabeth Lawrence	45
Wind Chimes	Macaque	48
On Reflection	Brenda Shrewsbury	51

Fantasy

The Mail-Order delivery	Elsa Heath	55
Lucy Comes Home	Fenja Hill	57
Daydreams	Elizabeth Lawrence	59
Feel My Pain	Louise Pople	61
Maud	Brenda Shrewsbury	64

Wall

Barriers	Elizabeth Lawrence	71
The Return	Elizabeth Lawrence	72
The Wall	Louise Pople	73

Menu

Best Friends Forever?	Fenja Hill	81
Language Enrichment	Elizabeth Lawrence	84
Menu	Macaque	86

Driftwood

Jetsam Coming Home	Jane Barron	91
Beach Treasures	Elizabeth Lawrence	93
If I Drift	Fenja Hill	95

Time

Time-slip	Jane Barron	99
An Idea of Heaven	Fenja Hill	102
Rhythms of Life	Elizabeth Lawrence	104
Schrodinger's Chronometer	Macaque	106
Dragon Story Time	Brenda Shrewsbury	110

Pride

Pride	Jane Barron	115
Cherry and Glory Pride	Lois Elsden	116
Two Haiku on the Theme of Pride	Sue Johnson	118
Northern Roots	Elizabeth Lawrence	119
The Seventh Deadly Sin	Brenda Shrewsbury	126

Wood

Stone Love	Sue Johnson	131
Renewal	Elizabeth Lawrence	132
The Nutcracker	Macaque	133

Haunting

Webs we Weave	Jane Barron	139
The Three Mummers	Lois Elsden	145
Haunting 101	Fenja Hill	147
The Silent Valley	Elizabeth Lawrence	149
Coventry Road	Macaque	152
Biographies		**161**
Index of Pieces		**166**
Index of Writers		**168**

Introduction

A summer's day in 2017, and a group of writers met for the first time in the Old Town Quarry in Weston-super-Mare, a now abandoned place which had given the town many of its fine Victorian buildings. A dozen or so writers sat outside the Rowan Tree Café, in glorious sunshine, planning their new writing group.

There were more than enough ideas, but first things first, and a name for the group… why did they want to be here, what did they want from being in a group… someone said they wanted '*a kick up the a**e to get writing!*' This seemed a splendid name, but they adopted the more inspirational title '*Writers in Stone*' since they were intending to have their meetings and share their work in the quarry. For various reasons, the group decamped to another meeting place, situated in the iconic old Tropicana Pool site, the Bay Café. The bay in question is Weston Bay, formerly Glentworth Bay, where for over two hundred years holiday makers have enjoyed the beach and the town's facilities.

Each month a topic is set – usually the writers look round, their minds vacant until they notice driftwood on the wall – the topic is Driftwood!...a menu – we'll write about Menus!...and of course, The Bay. They are a varied group of people with various writing histories and preferences, but one thing is not in question, their love of writing, their ability to write, and the quality of what they write…actually that is three things.

Now they have produced their first anthology, *Driftwood,* which they share with you here. Enjoy their work, be inspired, and if you're near Weston, join the Writers in Stone and have your writing *a**e* kicked!

Stories Inspired by a Photograph

A Definition of Excitement

Fenja Hill

I'm a bit worried. It's been fine so far; nobody's noticed anything out of place, and I have been able to visit every day without attracting attention. But today Kev reminded me that the beach racing is on next weekend, and that means they'll be digging up the dunes. Obviously, I knew she'd be found eventually, but I was thinking in terms of months, not weeks. Enough time for forensic evidence to degrade, for identification to become difficult, perhaps even impossible. I thought about Googling information about the rate of decomposition of bodies buried in sand, but I don't want to leave a trail on my laptop. I watch CSI and Bones, I know how they track this stuff down. I'll just have to hope that the forensic resources available in a small British seaside town are considerably less advanced than on US television.

Obviously, when it happened, I couldn't just leave her body lying out on the sand; people would have seen her and questions would have been asked immediately. Sooner or later, there would have been the proverbial knock at my door. After all, she had no friends, and she hadn't spoken to her family for months; I made sure of that. I was the only person she saw or spoke to, unless I sent her out to get beer or cigarettes and even then, she came straight home, didn't stop to chat or wander across to the tea-shop by the beach. She was well-trained. At least, I thought she was. That's why, as a special treat, I took her for a walk on the beach last Thursday evening. The best time is about sevenish, when everyone else is home having dinner. She was a bit hot in the jacket I made her wear, but some of the bruises were at that really vivid blue-green stage and people can be terrible for interfering.

I held her hand as we crossed the road. Important, because of that one time, when she was feeling a bit down and tried to run out in front of an Argos delivery lorry. Now, I make sure I remove the temptation. Just in case. We crossed to the beach and wandered, hand firmly in hand, southwards, towards Uphill beach. Fewer people that way; the tourists prefer to head north, towards the bright lights of the pier, the chip shops and bars.

The sunset was spectacular, as always. It lit her face, but it also lit up the marks on her neck, from yesterday's discussion about the correct way to iron a shirt.

That's when I discovered that she wasn't quite as well-trained as I had thought. As I stood in front of her, pulling the zip on her jacket up to hide the marks on her neck, I saw the outline of something in one of the pockets. Looking back up to her face, I knew that she had seen me looking at it, and I saw the fear in her eyes. I took my time sliding my hand into the pocket to find the betrayal hidden within.

All these months of teaching her, training her to be the good girl that I want, and for what? There in my hand, I was looking at a plastic library card and a bus ticket. A library card! Not only had she been going out behind my back, travelling into town on the bus, probably talking to strangers, making friends even, but somewhere in my house she was hiding books. There would be no need to have the card if she wasn't actually borrowing books, taking them home with her. All this, while I was out working to make the money to keep her; while I thought she was at home, keeping the house exactly as I like it, cooking my dinner, cleaning, waiting for me to come home to her.

Worse still, what if the books were *not* in my house? What if she had friends, had been visiting them, reading with them, keeping her books safe in their homes? Were they *men*? Was she having an affair?

To be honest, I did go over the top a bit. I don't usually punch her that hard when we're out; there's always the risk that she won't be able to walk home properly, that someone will notice. But I felt betrayed, cheated, and I lashed out without thinking. In some ways, she cheated me even then. My fist hit the side of her head so hard that I heard her neck snap. She crumpled to the sand and I knew, without checking, that she was dead. There was no pleasure in that; the pleasure would have come from teaching her a lesson, making sure she learned never to cheat me like that again. And she left me with the problem of getting rid of her body. It has occurred to me before that this could happen, after all, it wouldn't be the first time; but I always assumed I would be at home, where I would have the time and resources to get rid of her properly, like I did with Amanda.

The beach was empty, but sometimes the boy racers turn up in the evening to play chicken in their cars, daring one another to drive closer and closer to the sinking mud without getting bogged down, so I needed to move quickly.

That's why she's under that sand dune. Well, not exactly under it, more dug into the side. But I had to work with my hands, so I did the best I could. Funny though. In some ways I miss her. I find myself coming here every day, just for a walk, to look at the sunset; just to make sure she's still there, waiting for me to come home.

Now, I have four days before the diggers arrive, shifting tons of sand to create a course for the most exciting thing to happen on this beach each year. Until now, that is. Whatever happens to me when they find her, I know I will have completely redefined the local definition of exciting.

Uncle Pete

Elizabeth Lawrence

RNLI crew member and coxswain, he paused for a moment from boat inspection, and stood in typical pose – contemplative, eyes downcast as if bowing to a greater power and drawing on a pipe for certain, steadying comfort. Strong and even features of dark Spanish descent, set in a handsome, Cornish face, belie a modest and unassuming man; a man who ventured out in ferocious winds and stormy seas, risking his own life, alongside friends and crew members, to rescue a lifeboat in difficulty, on what was to become the night of the Penlee lifeboat disaster in 1981. The rescue attempt was unsuccessful and the boat turned back, 'leaking like a sieve', its occupants lucky to have escaped with their lives – boats sank and twelve men drowned that night.

The snapshot has caught a set, sober and distracted look, often worn by survivors of trauma, as he remembers mountainous waves, wailing winds and drowning men. Deservedly, in 1986, he was awarded a BEM for bravery and now lives every day in gratitude for the life he was spared; tending his garden and enjoying a pint at the local.

Hewn from a lifetime fishing along the treacherous Lizard coastline, he is also at peace with himself and the world around him – the deep blue sea, wide open spaces, ever changing weather, light and landscape; and the tranquillity of a peninsular.

A peaceful man, quietly content with where he was born and bred, he was one of five siblings, and the family grew all their own produce, kept chickens, and fish was the staple diet, with occasional meat from farming cousins. Friends, neighbours and families all looked out for each other, in the close knit, remote community, with the sea like a sparkling jewel, the air as pure and sweet as could be, and vibrant, dazzling colours from subtropical plants, deep blue skies, gulls, surf, brightly painted fishing boats and cottages – life was beautiful and he knew no other.

This man is Uncle Pete to my best friend. She is enormously proud of him, but finds it difficult to express, as he is so modest. The snapshot was taken by a card company and widely sold nationwide.

He was a gift with his film-star good looks, quietly hauling in ropes and nets – the real deal! Ever the reluctant hero, Uncle Pete has not received any revenue, and wouldn't want to. He also refuses to be interviewed; never drawn into superficiality and knowing the frailty of life; he is perfectly content.

Many a distressed damsel has fantasised about being rescued and carried to safety in those strong arms with head buried in his muscular chest! The air of slight detachment and dreaminess made him all the more appealing – this man would be dependable.

There are stories abounding about determined women capturing Uncle Pete; but he was always very honourable, in his compromised freedom.

Now aged eighty three, he seems to have regained a peaceful solitude, broken only by regular visits to his local for a pint and to his sister's each Sunday for a roast lunch.

Still a local hero, everyone remembers the Penlee Lifeboat disaster. He always took his lifeboat role very seriously and was highly regarded as the mechanic, as well as for his bravery.

Bride and Groom

Elizabeth Lawrence

They stood together, man and woman – vital, yet soft and tender. He, still handsome and his masculinity more an essence from his soul and memory – a response to her femininity; his partner through life; not in the once obvious muscular and easy confidence of the testosterone-fuelled days, but somehow, more assured and knowing – belonging to, and part of the love at his side. They were one, beautiful and poignant – she protective of him and the confusion of his mental frailty in later years; and he looking after her; a habit of a lifetime. Yin and Yang and finely honed. I felt very moved by the snap shot of these wedding guests; more beautiful, and emanating as much love as the bride and groom; but seemingly deeper, more tender and more sure of each other.

Ballet Rehearsal, 1873

Macaque

Degas sets up his easel at the end of the long room. Today he will paint the setting, capture in rough strokes the austere, grey background for the lithe, animated figures he has been sketching these past few weeks. It is a fresh, clear day in early December; snow lingers in the corners of the courtyard and the shade of the fir trees. The tall, arched windows let in a wash of the weak winter light, but the dancers cast hardly any shadow on the floor. The artist's keen eye observes them as they prepare, helping each other tie their bows neatly behind; stretching, graceful as swans, their thin, pale arms like slender necks, tutus like feathers floating on the dull lake of the floor. He sees every detail as his brush imitates the contrast between window and wall, sets the tone, creates the atmosphere.

He works swiftly, with unhurried ease, comfortable in his milieu; the girls and teachers at the Palais Garnier have learned to ignore him. They know it is the grace and beauty of the dance that interests him, the colour and movement of the dancers he loves, capturing the music and emotion of one art with the stroke and shade of another. He is a serious character, and a fine painter. He will make a name for himself, and perhaps for them too, the ones he singles out, brings to the foreground, elevates with a curious expression or a candid gesture. The painted girls will stay young long after their careers have ended.

Degas studies the sketches he has made; the pastel drawings of individual girls; of pirouettes, arabesques, pliés. He studies the girls warming up in the studio before him, watches the ones at the bar as well as those on the floor; his eyesight is strained, but he has a way of looking, of seeing the details, of knowing what has significance, what holds artistic truth. He has a sensitivity for beauty, for the artistic aesthetics of the everyday, and he amuses himself by including some of his observations, his *marginals*, in the wings of his canvases: two conspiring gents, dancers gossiping, a bored or tired girl leaning against a wall.

He sees Guillaume, the blind violinist, in his black greatcoat and dark grey trousers, black shoes wet with snow. Poor, tragic Guillaume; the girls seem to dance just for him; they pity and adore him for his affliction and his brilliance with the bow. He poses no threat, as they laugh and undulate before him, or remove their chemises and stockings: his loss of sight has emasculated him.

They say he plays to remember his wife who was a dancer. When she died he drank until absinthe and grief blinded him. Now, his head follows the movements of the girls, he hears the scuff and shuffle of their steps, senses the difference in the light as they twirl in front of the windows; he smiles as he plays for the dancing girls, lost in his memories.

But Degas sees the smudges of print ink on his fingers, and knows he reads the newspaper every day.

A Story in Fifty Words

50 Words about Fear

Macaque

Diego's moist palm palpated the knife's slender handle. He was nervous, but his mind was set; it had to be done, this act that was the hardest he had ever faced. Too late to worry about consequences; his fate was sealed. He readied the blade, and slit open the envelope.

Just a Trim

Louise Pople

He strutted into the hairdressing shop, an ageing peacock. Her young fingers ran through his greasy hair to the tip of his thinning ponytail. "Just a trim, gorgeous," his hand patted her bottom. He left no tip but she smiled, contented, scissors in hand, his ponytail limp on the floor.

The Proposal

Elizabeth Lawrence

He knelt before her, offering a ring. Silence descended, all attention on the man's earnestness and his love's embarrassed but beaming smile. She mouthed 'yes', keeping her hands in his, and as they kissed, a cork popped.

Shyness forgotten, they knew this scene would be replayed in their hearts, forever.

50 Words about Love

Macaque

All that pain
You caused, and she
Loved you: the loss of
Sleep, the worry, your frequent indifference,
All the times
You never listened, and still
She loved you.

And you met others
Who loved you
For a while, a lesser
Love, an imitation.

Then this;
And now you know.

The Bay

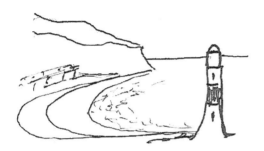

Lifelines

Elizabeth Lawrence

A spectator in a prime viewing seat, always at her post, positioned high, with the sun as a spotlight, she viewed her whole world from a bay window; and her world looked up at her. A lifelong early riser, optimistic and energetic – a 'true lark', she habitually still awoke at six, with the usual surge of life force, ready to take on any challenge, before the momentary crush of spirits, as reality dawned with the sunrise, and the realisation of her loss of freedom and autonomy hit her anew each morning.

Those first precious minutes were invaluable to adopting a mind-set for the day, and as an armour for dealing with the automaton nurse, on a conveyor belt of activity. Mavis needed to have decided upon her outfit and breakfast in advance; there would be no room for pondering and indecision – the normal luxuries of life. A plan had to be already in place, to dress and adorn herself with as much pride and pleasure as ever; not as vanity but for emphasis and expression; taking care over the details of matching scarves and brooches, her natural inclination towards vibrant colours to harmonise with the mood of the day. Once the nurse had dispensed with her timed bathing and dressing duties, Mavis patted silver curls into place and powdered porcelain skin, before adding cherry red lipstick to curve her ready smile and lift her whole face, to reach across even the dampest of misty days.

Breakfast was enjoyed as a highlight in the day, and love of food matched her appetite for life; a pleasure to be savoured, but always with an eye on the street.

The doctor's time-scale was too gloomy to dwell on and distracted her from the resolve not to enter the world of worry, illness and finality. She made a decision, to take life a day at a time and felt she could do this, for now, despite the effort costing more each day.

The nurse left abruptly with a resounding slam of the front door and strode down the path without a backward glance or wave at her imprisoned charge in solitary confinement. Mavis had long since given up expecting to reap what she had sown, in her own long and dedicated nursing career, and instead decided to join the ranks of those who grow old in peace and acceptance – far less wearing on the nerves; and a buffer against thoughtlessness.

Settled in her chair in the bay window, looking down and across her green and floral garden, allowing the luxury of surveying summer growth and young birds feeding as the garden basked in morning sun; shimmering spun gold across the dewy grass and shrubs. She made notes with exact instructions for the gardener, looking forward to his weekly task and being able to see her little patch transform. She had decided on wider flower borders, more plants, and the donkey statue moving to a lower wall, so that younger children could see over – they all loved the donkey with the basket of flowers on his back. The pond could do with weeding; it would be good to catch sight of the goldfish once again.

The garden was certainly colourful and eye-catching to passers-by, who often lingered and shared a smile of appreciation with the lady of the house. The lifelike donkey was a main feature that delighted children and adults alike; and stopping to wave was a ritual for many children on their way to and from school. Mavis ensured her world was as beautiful and interesting as her imagination and powers of persuasion could manage, in her allotted world of thirty square feet.

The first passer-by was usually the thin and anxious young mother, with an energetic, bright and demanding toddler bursting out of a pushchair. Sleep-deprived and just going through the motions of the day with no let-up, she looked forward to seeing the kindly and cheerful lady, who always appeared alert, enquiring and interested in her and her daughter. Mavis would laugh, wave, shake her head or give a sympathetic smile and a nod, as if she understood and was giving support and encouragement - someone who noticed changes, as if they mattered. Mavis was transported back in time to when her own daughter emigrated to Australia with a new baby; and all the ensuing long distance phone calls as Mavis tried to convey love and support from afar. 'Assisted Passage – assisted family breakup!' Mavis would grumble bitterly to her friends. And she made a shrine to her granddaughter, immortalised as a toddler, a halo of fluffy blonde hair and dimpled smile in a bejewelled photo frame.

A slower, more aimless pace brought a young man, drifting between the alleyways and doorways of life, with the occasional relief of soup kitchens (or even rarer, hostel beds), who came to look upon the silver haired old lady, raised up in her bay window, as a saintly mother figure, looking down so benevolently on him, so that he felt understood for the first time in his life, and warmed by her smile as their eyes met for a few seconds, hers with questioning, motherly concern and a nod of recognition for his struggle, which was succour to his soul, meeting his need. As she raised her hand to wave, the tinkling sound of her loose wedding rings surprised her – they used to fit so snugly against her firm, smooth flesh, glinting with her animated hand movements, and set off with manicured and painted nails. She didn't recognise the bony fingers and wrinkled skin as her own.

Where was her wayward son now? She hungered to know – always so headstrong and bent on self-destruction, as he followed various passions and causes, which led him to an underworld, where he cut family ties. *'When does the mother bond break and the young seek others?'* she mused; and would die happy at the sight of him walking up the road, coming home.

A shabby, elderly man, stooped against the ravages of life, in a mismatch of handout clothes, accustomed to blank or derisory faces, long since having given up hope of a *'good day'* or a passing comment on the weather, looked forward to the waves from this warm-hearted mother figure, who appeared to care about, and know him as the misunderstood, lonely and unfortunate man he was. She reflected sunshine and he imagined soft chairs, plump cushions, a warm fire as she softly hummed, toasting tea cakes and pouring tea. These were very distant memories of his own mother, which ended before his sharp memory had developed. Alone in austere digs, each and every day the most important task was to walk past the bay window and feel blessed, warmed and comforted by *'the smile'.*

And Mavis thought of her own very dear, departed husband and his muddled last years, as he looked to her as his guide and compass, navigating a world he no longer recognised; shabbily dressed, stooped and bewildered, bearing no resemblance to the striking and strong man she had married and enjoyed raising a family with; but still finding time to enjoy life together. Always the stronger, Mavis knew she would be alone at the end.

And so the weeks trundled by over months and seasons. The daily, renewable energy of the passers-by, hurriedly and purposely en route, contrasted sharply with the wasting figure of Mavis; turning into a husk of her once vibrant, human form; and most were unaware that she withered with the autumn leaves; but would not renew or return. The daily connection to the world was lifeblood to Mavis, and she dreaded the inevitable retreat into the dark capsule of the back bedroom, where she hoped the journey down the dark tunnel would be swift.

The winter was harsh and it became too arduous for most to go out – dark days, lashing winds, bitterly cold with deep snow, treacherous under foot, until late winter sunlight brought a thaw.

The toddler, now skipping and jumping excitedly, raced up to the low walled garden in search of the donkey and the cheery wave of attention; and she stopped in her tracks. Her mother discovered why her daughter was uncharacteristically still, as she scanned a neglected, overgrown garden, devoid of the donkey; and glancing up at the bay window, met her worst fears – the room was dark and empty.

The Sunfold

Macaque

Gazing at the wide bay
From the wide bay window,
Along the polished sill of the horizon
I watch the sun fold into the sea
Like a crimson kiss

And I wonder what it's like
To be endlessly, faultlessly
Loved like this

The Bay

Louise Pople

She never considered herself to be an artist, she was just someone who liked to paint. When others referred to her as an artist, she felt embarrassed, as there was no way that she could live up to such a grand title. An artist was somebody with talent and creativity, but she could never see those traits in herself even though others saw them in her. She never saw anything good in herself or her art and, these days, saw little good in others. As she sat on her canvas stool on the side of the sand dune, her colours set out in front of her, browns and greys and blues that she so often worked with, she looked down to the bay, her eyes scanning the beach, the sea and the headland, patiently waiting to see what would catch her eye, where her brush would make its first mark on the canvas.

He sat behind the rocks on the headland, staring intently at the incoming tide. A kind caring man, with hands that bore the scars of his work on the land. A lonely man who had spent a lifetime secretly loving the artist, always too shy, too nervous to approach her. What would an artist want with a humble flower grower? He watched her wrap her oversized cardigan around herself and sink into its warmth and he thought about how he had dreamed a thousand times of wrapping his arms tightly around her slight frame and having her sink into his embrace. He painted a picture in his mind of their life together, in the warm vivid comforting hues of autumn, a picture of not just what their lives might have been but what they could be.

The bay was deserted, as it so often was at this time of year. The artist was used to emptiness, that's how she had lived her life since her parents had passed away. She kept herself to herself; after all who would be interested in talking to a boring old woman like her? If no one had found her the least bit interesting in the last 72 years they weren't going to be interested in her now.

After several minutes of taking in her surroundings, her eyes were drawn to the shoreline where she could see a small silver cylinder being rolled onto the beach and then being dragged back into the waves. Backwards and forwards it rolled completely at the mercy of the incoming tide. She wondered about whether to make her way from her viewpoint on the sand dune down on to the beach. She thought that by the time she reached the cylinder it may be swept out to sea by a wave and all her efforts would have been for nothing. "I wonder what it could be?" she muttered to herself. The cylinder rolled further up the beach and then away again each time being sucked back towards the headland. *It's no good*, she thought I'm going to have to take a closer look.

Her boots slid deep into the soft sand as she ran down the steep side of the dune. On reaching the flat she covered the ground quickly and easily down to the harder rippled sand below and on to the tide line. With each surge the sea raced up to her feet but with careful timing she chased the tide back, grabbing the cylinder with her hand, turning and running as fast as she could back towards the dunes before the next wave could overtake her. She stopped on the dry sand away from the tormenting waves and looked closely at the cylinder. It had been shiny at one time but was now dull and battered and scratched. Turning it over she noticed a name engraved in the metal: Lottie Wood. Her hands started to tremble. Lottie Wood, that was her name, well Charlotte Wood, nobody had called her Lottie since she was a child. She struggled back up the sand dune, each step being heavier than the last, until, exhausted and quite shaken, she sat on her small canvas stool, got out her reading glasses and took a closer look at the object in her hand. It wasn't so much a metal cylinder but a metal vacuum flask, she tried to unscrew the top, but it was too tightly closed. Reaching into her artist's box she pulled out a metal palette knife and prized the top off and was then able to unscrew the lid. She held the flask at arm's length and tipped its contents out in front of her.

Almost immediately, out of the flask slipped a deep red rose. A rose so fresh that it could have been picked that morning. The dew was still on its velvet petals. She picked up the rose and held it under her nose taking in the deep heavy aroma of the flower. Attached to the stem with a piece of green twine was a card which read "I have loved you since I first set eyes on you and if you will allow me, I shall love you for the rest of my life."

Her heart pounded in her chest as it had never done before, she felt dizzy and confused. Her hands shook, and tears welled in her eyes. Oh, how she had wanted someone to love her, oh how long she had waited for someone to say these words to her. A lifetime of waiting, a lifetime of yearning. She looked around her, but the cove was deserted. She didn't understand, she felt confused. *Someone must be playing a joke* she thought, *a silly nasty practical joke. How could anybody love her?* She stared at the rose, gripping it tightly in her hand, its sharp thorns drawing blood from her fingers, it dropped at her feet and pushing it with the heel of her boot it sank deeper and deeper into the soft sand. Sucking the blood off her fingers she packed up her stool and grabbed her opened artists' box spilling the tubes of paints in her rush and marched indignantly away from the bay, back through the marram grass towards the village.

The elderly flower grower hiding in the rocks by the headland had seen all of this. He retrieved his walking stick that he had used to push the old flask around the rocks and into the current, heaved a heavy sigh, picked his way back over the rocks and pebbles and walked slowly back in the opposite direction towards his cottage.

On the sand dune above the bay lay the tubes of discarded paints, reds, oranges, yellows and bright vermillion, which could have painted a thousand beautiful sunsets.

Euphonic Writing

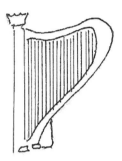

This is the entrance lock to the Manchester and Salford Junction Canal...

Lois Elsden

When we first came to Manchester, many years ago, it was a buzzing city, even then, but there were still many areas of neglect - including bomb sites left over from the war which hadn't yet been cleared and rebuilt. The rivers and canals were similarly neglected, filthy in places, disgusting and clogged with rubbish as well as weeds. Derelict waterways which had once been thriving and busy routes into thriving and busy industrial areas - mills, factories, wharfs, docks, warehouses - were like the sewers of the city.

Now they have been given new life; not only is the water clean and fishermen cast their lines along the banks, leisure craft of every shape, size and sort, enjoy the freedom of travelling through the city and out into the countryside and beyond, but for the walker there are accessible paths and walks alongside with pubs, cafés and hostelries bustling and busy.

Look down, past the lime sprig of buddleia, and the lock gates are ajar. The water is white with the sky and you could swim through the reflected clouds, and through the reflection of a metal bridge carrying a pipeline, swim through into the water beyond, the Irwell.

This is the entrance lock to the Manchester and Salford Junction Canal... the so-called forgotten canal; if you walk over the bridge, in either direction, you descend to a path, towards the river. The edge of the lock is now punctuated by posts, link-chained. The water could be ice, reflecting like a mirror the pipe-line bridge, power cables unseen except on the surface of the lock.

It has hidden depths, in many ways; its history not remembered, its workers long forgotten, its builders who even were they?

What lies beneath, who knows?

The image is bordered by autumn trees, maybe a birch, golden and green, maybe a pine, dark, its branches lifting in praise or surrender, and beneath, wild foliage, surrounding a lamp, maybe a gate to Narnia.

Beyond the Irwell, the city, glimpsed beneath the metal arms of some feature of the lock gate, a tall upright structure, to lift, to turn, to open? - the city beyond, in the fading distance has the dim red shapes of buildings, maybe a church, maybe a Lowryesque mill, maybe now a modern hotel; imagination can make of it anything!

This is the entrance lock to the Manchester and Salford Junction Canal...

Yin and Yang

Elizabeth Lawrence

Well! What happened, was – the alarm clanged and clamoured, causing consternation in her cluttered consciousness. She *so* needed a voluptuary awakening; to snuggle, snooze and shuffle in the downy duvet, desiring to delectably dream, to revive, renew, beautify, bolster and balance the mind. Muffled into plush pillows, she sighed and soothed in spoonfuls. Feeling floaty, she eased and elongated herself out of bed, eased her feet into fluffy mules; and wrapped her sleep-warmed body in a fleecy gown, following the aromatic aroma of smoky caramel coffee. Hands clasping the warming elixir of comfort, clarity, composure, spirit and zest – yes, zest! Zest kicked in with a zing and a need to zip and zoom to meet a forbearing and forgiving friend. After a shower, shake and lather, she chasséed and shimmied into shimmering, glimmering, glittering, glamorous, feathery finery.

Soon to meet, greet and sparkle in the springtime; but the immediate, imploring, messaging world, lured, pulled and tempted her to peer at enticing posts and surprises, to feel connected to the universe, with all the needy, niggling nuances of humanity, with occasional bursts of inspiration; and couldn't resist rococo replies!

An orbiting magnet of salutations, felicitations, solutions and strength, her world was heavy with feeling filings. So, she filed and fled, frittering fripperies with a frisson of frisettes; on a thermal of thoughts and in thrall of a cornucopian morn: dewy, glistening, listening, glimpsing honeyed rays through trees, dripping onto buttercups. She stopped and stalled, as sea sirens held her senses and sang to her soul. Rocks ricocheted, shells echoed and crunched, as shingles on the shore swished and swooshed, washing away mortal mundane, hearing timeless, ancient callings ....callings? Chords struck, heart strings pulled, towing the line, safe harbour-home, followed her star, anchored mooring, heeded the need and found her friend!

The brick wall loomed, and his only view, a huge functional wall clock, chiming the quarters away, locked him into his waiting room. He stewed and studied the time, intently, as if trying to solve a tricky puzzle, looking down the lonely well of a half empty mug of cold coffee. Acting in a make-believe meeting, in a mocking charade but fooling no one. He chose not to face the busy, bustling park of happy people with jocular, jarring voices, loving couples, children and dogs abounding, and abundant spring growth, sprouting daily; a fixed, closed mind ever recalling, recoiling and shrinking into fenced-off thoughts. He waited, and was reminded of tethered dogs outside shop doorways, anxious and intent on their owner's return; oblivious to the friendly reassurances and distractions of others. The need for his friend was overwhelming and greater than anything.

The door finally burst open and his friend stood before him with concerned, gentle twinkling eyes, filling his vacuum with laugher, colour and warmth; and he felt connected to the world again, as he waited for her devotion, emotion and commotion, in oceans of sympathy and empathy. He listened readily to her elaborate excuse, basking in her expressions and cadences, and felt himself becoming alive with the yin and yang of them, as he absorbed her, and she recharged in his quiet, consuming presence.

She was his whole universe and sometimes her world was just too big.

The Bone-Yard

Macaque

Chain links swing, clink,
Sing in the wind, wink
In the shine, the rusting spine
Climbing high to the hook-head.

Rough ropes spool in pools of oil,
Coil in the dirt, skirt drums
That burst, splay, spray dark
Ichor in the heart of the bone-yard.

A shock of broken spokes pokes
Through split tarpaulin skin.
Rooted in dust, the rusting wrecks'
Twisted necks and limp limbs

Lie listless and lost, tossed in
Heaps, wind-sweeps, sly piles
Of smashed tiles, ruptured veins of
Wire waving tattered flags of snagged rags

In the twilight grime,
In the bone-yard, where the
Chain links swing, clink, sing
In the wind, wink in the shine…

Reflections

Mirror Images

Elizabeth Lawrence

Reflections: a soft sounding word, drawn out and inviting a pause to ponder .....

Quietly reflecting on reflections, I thought 'what a beautiful concept a reflection is.' As the imagination drifts to iconic scenes over water, such as snow-capped mountains under blue skies with white clouds; the symmetrical grace of swans, elongating and curving their necks over depths of still water – an eternally tranquil scene. Canadian trees in the fall, with their warming reds and golds, reflecting onto mirror-like lakes; glorious sunsets through dramatic clouds, over a motionless sea, all capture a perfect replica of the original, doubling the pleasure.

And then indoor reflections, such as capturing flames from a fire, reflected in brass or copper; candles reflecting in glass holders, and festooned fairy lights over glass doors reflect, seemingly endless, mirrored, magical tunnels of lights.

I often mentally reflect, perhaps too often, scenes and conversations can be replayed almost exactly, reflecting the original, sometimes painfully, angrily, beautifully, humorously, or delightfully. Too much reflecting can be a hindrance to living in the present, and lead to dwelling or obsessing on a subject, which I have a tendency to do! Reflection should be transitory, like a brief image in nature – a moment of insight or joy.

How often do we see reflections of ourselves in others, who may return the warmth of our smile, share a sad moment, empathise and comfort with a lingering softness in the eye, reflecting between two people. A loving look, unmistakeable, instinctive and learned from infancy.

Those with a faith speak of reflecting the Son of God in their demeanour and countenance; and as they look on His face, the reflection becomes theirs – a beautiful concept. We can find ourselves continually reflecting role models and heroes in our lives, as they live on through us.

I first encountered the power of a reflection a few months after my mother died, as I unconsciously searched for her everywhere; looking at lifeless photographs, still and frozen in time; empty chairs, silent rooms, a phone that didn't ring anymore, and her voice gone forever. Sometimes, in moments of despair, I would look in the mirror, as if trying to fill a void by seeing a living, expressive face, albeit it only mine. As I looked, deeply and searchingly, into my own eyes, I was struck by the similarity of colour to my mother's; blue-grey with a warm brown ring around the pupil, which I always thought gave depth and kindness to her expression. With the pleasing memory, my eyes took on movement and excitement and my mother's eyes looked back at me, speaking through her gaze, a language I knew, instinctively – no longer my eyes, but my mother's, holding me in her strong, steady and reassuring gaze. We had been so close, and often didn't need words – a look could say it all - and now my mother's eyes spoke of infinite love and the certainty of life going on, now as before. I was spellbound – the reflection was not my own, anymore. This now occurs regularly, whenever I have time to reflect. Sometimes, if I'm amused about something, my mother's eyes dance with laughter, as we share jokes and irony. And she still gives me that very 'knowing look'!

I then expanded my reflection experience to my grandmother, after catching her reflection from windows in the dark when the house was lit up; a similarity of smile and profile and then her face came to life. I am comforted by the female trinity still around me – my grandmother, mother and I were known as "three peas in a pod", and the affinity continues as I sometimes catch my mother in my daughter's expression or stance. Perhaps a sign that psychic energy doesn't die.

In my reflections, I must mention that important, frivolous backward glance in the mirror before going out, adjusting a hat, swishing a scarf to best effect and confirmation that a colour works, gaining reflected energy and positivity as a confidence boost to greet the world.

Reflections are necessary in life – the pace can be too fast. Research has shown that daydreaming reduces stress and is good for the brain, as it takes time out from immediate and repetitive thought processes, the brain repairs and produces renewed energy and creativity.

Sometimes reflecting on past actions or words can give us the chance to make different choices, take new opportunities or change direction.

And sometimes, it's the special moments in life that make our memories – and are wonderful to relive, as we take time to reflect.

Wind Chimes

Macaque

The deep shade of the veranda was still cool, the susurrating nocturnal dampness still perceptible, but the breeze that brought the heady throb of insects from the olive grove was warm and dry, and the most beautiful part of the day would soon be gone. Mary looked up from her work and across the pale, coarse grass to the trees, a sombre chiaroscuro in the middle distance before the sun-baked cliffs dropped to the vibrant blue water, already glaring in the mid-morning light. Soon the day would be consumed by the unrelenting Mediterranean heat. She embroidered a couple of stitches, then, with a sigh that echoed the olive breeze, set the work down on the sewing basket beside her. She rose and went inside to fetch a glass of lemonade.

The cool, cloudy liquid was a double comfort in the arid hours she spent alone here. It reminded her of England, of her childhood picnics and the croak of frogs across the village green. She took a long, nostalgic draught and crossed the bare floor of the living room to the open window. A blue vase on the sill caught the morning light and refracted it beautifully, playfully. That blue vase: so much a piece of home in this alien setting. Tom had given it to her on his return from Italy. She kept seasonal flowers in it all year round, sliding the stems past the gaping beak and down the slender neck as if she were feeding a fledgling. She adored its functional elegance, but today the vase was empty. Setting down her glass, she picked up the vase, so touchingly silent in its hunger. Mary's eyes stared squarely through the open window, but her gaze was inward. The blue sky, the coarse grass and the glinting wave crests ceased to register, taken for granted as the sensation of shoes around accustomed feet.

She was putting a sprig of mistletoe into the blue glass vase in London. The mantelpiece was festooned with garlands of pine cones tied with red ribbon. The red woollen stockings were hanging from the brass candle holders either side of the mirror, and Tom was right, of course, that the vase didn't suit the mantle at Christmas, but she smiled as she stepped back from the hearth, pleased with her creation. She smoothed the flames' heat from her dress. The mistletoe fanned out beautifully in front of the mirror, and the polished vase swirled with the shadows from the fire. She poured two glasses of sherry and placed them next to the vase. The scene was set. Tom would be home soon.

The pale brown face of a local boy intruded upon her dreams; one of the children from the village along the coast, whom she often saw passing through the olive grove. It was a face she had seen many times in the distance, fixing her with a curious, kind gaze, much less of a stare because of its innocence. She thought sometimes that she also detected yearning in the features, and in the way that, smaller than the other boys, he straggled, seemed less a part of the gang. This familiarity notwithstanding, at such close quarters and appearing so suddenly, the boy's face startled her, assaulted the senses of sight and sound and touch, breaking her reverie and making her aware once again of her present surroundings. Her breath froze for an instant. As the child's head pushed into the aperture of the window her lungs contracted and froze there, contracted, for an instant. As the boy's head intruded and her lungs contracted, her arms, in perfect syncopation, expanded; her fingers lingering on the threshold of reality released the vase they seemed not to be holding. As the brown face of the curious child rose up into the view of the dreamer, the blue vase, the phial of dreams, fell, in counterbalance, to the cold tiled floor.

The shattering sound was what she heard first. The seconds retraced themselves when the space inside the vase was already greater than the surface area of the glass. In the instant that followed the noise, she saw the face, she saw the smile, she saw the fingers expand and the vase fall, and already the boy had disappeared. The ensuing silence was overpowering. Her heart was beating louder and faster than the crickets, and she felt gripped, squeezed by the contrast of brightness and shade as she remained frozen in front of the window, unable to move, flushed with adrenaline and disbelief. The knocking continued for several seconds before the spell was broken.

The knocking was now quite urgent. Perhaps someone had heard the shattering of glass and was calling out of concern. The reality of the incident seemed so trivial as she hastened to the front door, readying an apology for causing alarm. But it was no-one she expected to see; not one of the near neighbours nor any of the locals who tended the gardens. She was greeted by the face of no-one she knew. Beyond this strange young man with the serious expression, away from the shade of the eaves, the day was now unbearable. She gazed beyond him as he spoke, gazed through him as he delivered the news, gazed past the stone wall and the dusty road at the dry hills that shimmered in the remorseless sunlight. There had been an accident; he was sorry; it was Tom; was there anything he could do; he really was dreadfully sorry.

How long she stood there, for how long the poor messenger spoke, she knew not. Sense, reason and time had all been consumed by the heat, together, in the single smashing of a glass vase. Her mind was busy associating images from the past, gathering fragments of her life together to try to make sense of the words, of the present. Finally composed, she gently closed the door and returned to the living room in a state of calm shock. Feeling numb and cumbersome, she sat herself down in a wicker chair that faced the screen door onto the veranda. Still in a daze, her gaze drifted over the shaded tapestry, gently billowing where it had come unhooked, to the open window with the lemonade glass on the sill. Flies were swooping round it wetting their feet on its sticky rim. How she detested the sound of flies. But she was becoming aware of another, strange sound, a bright, celestial sound. And there was something glinting against the clear sky where it bordered the dark recess of the room. The pieces of the smashed vase had been tied carefully with thread and pinned with embroidery needles to the wooden frame. She thought once more of the boy with the curious, brown, face, and with her broad, gentle smile, the tears came.

On Reflection

Brenda Shrewsbury

The words and phrases slammed into her like bullets, her body swaying at each impact. Deliberation, culpable, probability, evidence, manifestation, due consideration and then the clincher "on reflection".

On Reflection. On reflection. On reflection. It hammered into her brain. Would she, with the wonder of hindsight have acted differently? If she had the luxury of time could she have reflected on her actions, made other choices? Would there have been a different outcome? As the words continued to wash over her, swirling away from conscious recognition, her mind wandered over the events that had brought her to this.

It was a dark and windy night; realisation of the cliché made her smile. Was her smile observed? Would it count against her? She hoped not. She shivered, her body responding even now with those primal instincts. A prickle of fear dashed up her spine and landed firmly in her gut. Suddenly she was alert, senses heightened, the hairs on the back of her neck literally standing up. So was that the moment she could have made a different choice? Should those little hairs have shown her another path, made her quicken her step, told her to scream as if her lungs would burst?

She swayed, toppling forward, balance almost gone, breaths quickening, a small sob breaking free from her mouth. Was that then or now? She could no longer tell. Body and mind separated, was that the way to stay safe? Let your mind take flight, while your body is rooted in the here and now of fear. For she was afraid, very afraid both then and now.

What had made her split the cost and the drinking of that third bottle of wine? She knew she needed a clear head for the presentation she was to give the following day. Choosing to walk off home across the heath to clear her head, to ward off the horrors, the unprofessionalism of a hangover on a Wednesday morning.

She knew how much her chance of promotion was tied into her moments of glory on that podium. She had been as prepared as it was possible to be; yet, yet she had allowed herself to be seduced by her friends, the ambience of the wine bar and a pair of laughing eyes.

Perhaps it was her anxiety to seem always to be in control, no signs of nerves to be displayed before or during the event. The need to appear to be perfect and in control when she knew deep in her soul, the soul she did her very best to keep hidden from everyone, that it took little to tip her into panic when challenged. Her anxious beast within, the one, if cornered in argument be it academic or emotional would ensure she came out fighting. Then there were her rages; oh how hard she had fought over the years to ensure that part of her was tamped - indeed stamped - down.

It was that beast of rage that came hurtling out of her as the hand landed on her shoulder, the heavy breathing soft on her cheek as he swung her round. It was the rage that came out of her with such force that she struck him full on the nose, breaking it instantly and as they fell to the ground it was her rage that kept her pummelling, pummelling his face into the ground. If it had not been for strong hands pulling her away she would have continued till every last breath had left both their bodies. She would have continued, never seeing his laughing eyes or her gloves, that he had been trying to catch up with her to deliver.

She could feel the pain in her hands now, looking down, though there was no blood, no bruising no broken bones. Her knuckles glowed white with the pain from gripping onto the rail of the dock.

She was back in the present, the jurors' stares showing, disquiet, disgust, pity and then the judges words started to register in her brain. 'On reflection" he agreed with the jury decision, 'manslaughter not murder' but, on reflection, she and her rage knew otherwise.

Fantasy

The Mail-Order Delivery

Elsa Heath

Ivy and David Franklin sat transfixed, as the green line ate up the time until the new chapter of their lives would begin. Ivy could hardly breathe. The waves of excitement had fizzled in her stomach ever since she'd woken up that morning, but now that they were there in the waiting room, those feelings had been clawed back by spasms of doubt.

Had they done everything correctly... in the right order? She was sure they had forgotten something; the process had been so rushed. Everything always did take forever unless you were one of the privileged few in the upper classes. Still they'd planned everything carefully to allow for complications: making lists and checking each item off...and that was before they'd even looked at any of the paperwork.

Ivy smiled as she remembered the day the message had come through. She'd kept swiping feverishly at the calendar on the wall, just in case she'd muddled up the date. So Ivy didn't initially hear the familiar chime announcing the arrival of post. By the time she'd skidded into the kitchen, David was already peering at the letter; his reading glasses were askew and his finger tracing the air in front of him. She had hastily put on her glasses and skimmed the projected Notification. The hologram in front of them momentarily slipped out of view as Ivy and David embraced, scarcely able to believe what they'd read: the forms had finally arrived.

Ivy remembered David's hands trembling as he caught the pile of papers which were pushing themselves through the small rectangular hatch set into the kitchen wall. They gazed at the documents which were stamped with the traditional image of a stork, as if they might self-combust at any moment. Those pink and blue sheets were the first step towards their dream of becoming parents: they had to complete them perfectly.

The next few weeks after that were a flurry of activity, as they raced to get everything ready. There were so many questions on the form, ranging from the mundane (What is your preferred eye colour for your child? Select from blue, brown, green or grey. Hazel and amber are available for the upper classes only) to the nerve-wracking (choose up to eight flaws for your child: quick-tempered, arrogant, overly-sensitive, forgetful, prone to insomnia…). They found that upper-class members had reserved most of these in an effort to secure the least damaging traits so Ivy and David had been left with forgetfulness or insomnia. After many late night discussions, the couple had settled on forgetfulness because both conceded they got very grumpy when deprived of sleep! Finally they had finished and eagerly returned the now crumpled pages of their future.

Surprisingly, it hadn't taken long for the documents to be approved and now it was the big day at last. The green line on the progress monitor inched ever closer to the 'Installation Complete' icon…three…two…one…the icon suddenly pulsed scarlet as if tasting life for the first time.

"Time for you to meet your daughter. Would you both like to cut the cord?"

Ivy and David jumped. They had been so mesmerised by the progress monitor that they had completely forgotten about the Technical Engineer who was there to oversee the process. Ivy smiled weakly as she looked into the woman's kind face and took the small blade offered to her.

As if driven by instinct, she placed her hand on top of David's and together they sliced through the red ribbon which was tied across a wide chute next to the monitor. For a few seconds nothing happened and then a beautiful baby slid down the chute into the Engineer's waiting hands. Beaming, she handed her to Ivy who already had tears of joy rolling down her face. She gazed into her daughter's perfect eyes for the first time: grey eyes exactly like they had chosen.

"What are you going to call her?" asked the Engineer.

Ivy and David smiled at each other. Question 4a had been the hardest on the form but now it seemed as if it had been made just for its new owner.

"Rosalind".

Lucy Comes Home

Fenja Hill

Closing the door of her penthouse apartment behind her, Lucy sat down on the leather footstool placed just inside for exactly this purpose, dropped her briefcase on the floor, kicked off her Jimmy Choos, carefully rolled down and removed each of her stockings, then stood and wriggled her toes on the soft Afghan wool of the rug, before throwing her jacket onto the sofa and heading for the drinks cabinet. She really should hang the jacket carefully and put her shoes away in the beautiful teak shoe cupboard that she had had fitted last month; after all between them the jacket and shoes had cost almost two thousand pounds. She couldn't be bothered though. Tired from a long day of meetings and presentations, all geared towards making sure that her company's final bid to take over their biggest rival would be successful, all she wanted was to pour herself a drink and relax in warm, scented bubble bath.

On another day, she might have called Maria as she left the office, and her bath would have been ready by the time she got home, but she had given Maria the day off, so she would just have to run the bath herself. She would have to order in some food, too, because a quick scan of the kitchen indicated that Maria hadn't bothered to shop this week. Lucy would have to have words with her tomorrow, make sure she didn't make that mistake again.

She lingered over the choice between wine and whisky, eventually selecting a crystal tumbler and pouring herself a generous helping of the Macallan Rare Cask that she had been saving for a special occasion. She carried it through to the bathroom and set it down at the side of the bath, then spent a few minutes adjusting the temperature of the water and the power and direction of the jets, before dimming the light and turning on some soft music.

Lucy removed her clothes, stepped into the bath and lifted the tumbler to her lips.

***

When the police finally decided to take the increasingly frantic calls from Mrs Porter seriously, and broke into the scruffy basement bedsit in Finsbury Park, the first one through the door tripped over an upturned wooden orange crate, skidded on a pair of tatty trainers immediately inside the door and landed hard on the bare wooden floor. His face was protected to some extent, by a grubby track-suit top lying in a heap with a pair of socks, a little further inside. The second officer through the door picked up a pile of papers that had been lying next to the trainers. Job Centre records of posts applied for, a number of letters, all on the theme of "we regret to inform you ….." and a copy of a rather sparse CV.

There was no sign of the young woman they were looking for, and the room was small enough to take in at one glance. A mattress and duvet against one wall, a small table and a single chair against another. In what appeared to be the kitchen area, the door of the only cupboard hung open and the contents were easy to see. A bag of sugar and a packet of cornflakes; one plate, one bowl and a few items of cutlery. There was no cooker or microwave and no refrigerator.

The first officer had found his feet and was trying to put his ignominious fall behind him, so he decided to show some initiative, and walked to the only other door, pulling it open and stepping inside.

Lucy lay in about six inches of water, in the stained and chipped bathtub. There was a cracked coffee mug with "World's greatest daughter" written on it, resting on her stomach. Later examination would show that it had contained household bleach, which explained the state of her lips and mouth. The young officer didn't recognise the gadget lying on the floor beside the bath, but his older colleague explained that it was a Walkman, there would be a CD inside it. They could see that it was playing, seemingly on repeat. He gently removed one of the headphone leads from Lucy's ear and held it close to his own, making out, through the tinny echoes, the theme from Mash.

Daydreams

Elizabeth Lawrence

When do we start having fantasies, assuming everyone does? Perhaps they are present from birth, or in the womb; who knows – they are just daydreams, after all.

My first memory of a fantasy was at the age of two, when I had a close and constant companion, named Goldilocks. Her hair, as the name suggests, hung in shiny, golden ringlets, framing her round cheeks and beaming face. I like to think she was my guardian angel, but perhaps that is just another fantasy. She was as real to me, then, as my baby sister became a year later, when Goldilocks disappeared. But in the meantime, Goldilocks didn't leave my side and, actually taking physical space, would squeal as people sometimes sat on her, mistaking her for an empty seat – very distressing for me! Perhaps she was my alter ego – the person I saw as me; and very good natured about taking the blame for my occasional misdeeds; or rather, the trivia adults made a fuss about. I remember the comfort of someone just like me; the same size and age, always at my side to counter the isolation of being a single child in a family of adults; often misunderstood or uncomprehending; perhaps fantasies stem from need.

Always a dreamer, with a need to wander, I frequently went missing, taking my doll in her pushchair to the doctors', along a busy road; or joining strangers' garden tea parties and picnics, uninvited, but unable to resist the temptation of such delectable sights as I passed by. Reality always arrived with a bump as my mother raced to claim me and I became a small child again!

I started school well enough and seemed to manage day to day, alongside daydreaming, until the age of eight when a mysterious illness necessitated long periods in bed with fluctuating fevers. We lived at the top of a hill, the highest point of a fishing village, and clouds and mist would roll in across the sea, rising up from the valley, borne on prevailing winds. From a sick-bed, my only view was the sky, and clouds became my whole world; a kingdom of swirling, spiralling, billowing vapours of snowy mountain ranges, candy-floss, magic carpets and plump pillows. Sledges and chariots (I'd been reading Ben Hur!) drawn by dogs or horses scurried across the sky.

Like Egyptian gods, lions and cats with huge faces and bodies appeared and disappeared, evolving and metamorphosing into unicorns or elephants. Faces of angels with towering wings, and whole armies advanced as storm clouds gathered and the celestial world changed from blue skies and dazzling, white fluffy clouds, to ominous dark grey, sometimes vibrant, indigo or black, with the brilliance of sunlight before a storm or deluge. The sky was so powerful and huge as I lay, waiting in wonder, watching clouds journey, seeing faces and forms so distinctly. The speed of their travel allowed for stories and fantasies - some slow and some rapid; but always dreamy, mesmerising and peaceful.

Reality meant frequent house calls from the doctor, baffled by a child not recovering and prescribing countless antibiotics, which I usually spat out, gagging on the bitter taste. And overhearing my mother say she feared I would have been "pushing up daisies" by now. Adults said strange things which made my fantasy world all the more appealing.

As I drifted in and out of sleep, (too poorly to read and no daytime TV nor playing in the house - conversations or quiet being the norm) the sound of school children at playtime rose from the valley and seemed to ascend with the clouds to my bed. I could hear the energy, excitement and lively chatter. The laughter and Cornish accents became part of my dreams, as my spirit seemed to move among the thriving children.

Despite becoming very thin and being carried up to bed most evenings in a delirious sleep, I survived the three months of illness, and look back on that time as a period of deep, inward peace – unaware of my parents' anxiety and the doctor's pessimism. I feel that my fantasies led me to health, perhaps supported and protected on a fluffy cloud of angels.

Fantasies are still a life-raft and safety valve; and my head is still mostly in the clouds; more fascinating than on the ground; with the exception of the ocean but that is a whole other fantasy story!

Feel my pain

Louise Pople

Mrs Butler sat staring at the computer in front of her. The download box in the centre of the screen flashed menacingly, whilst the timer counted down: 54,53,52,51. She knew that if she didn't act quickly, her one and only chance to download the browser onto the dark web would be gone. 42, 41, 40, 39. Her finger hovered over the enter key. 22, 21, 20, 19. She wanted to close the lid of the laptop but something stopped her, was it fear or excitement? 11, 10, 9, 8. Now her index finger was shaking and her heart thumping inside her chest. She thrust her finger onto the key. The screen blanked and then flashed "Pandora is installing" She took a large breath of air into her lungs and leant back into her chair, rubbing her eyes and pushing her glasses onto her head. A menu screen appeared in front of her. She scanned the search bar. The word Magic jumped out at her, Black Magic, she read "The use of supernatural powers for evil purposes." Her heart quickened as she pressed the enter key. She knew that she may be getting out of her depth but these days it wasn't uncommon to hear that people had used black magic against someone who had wounded them, and the wounds that her husband had dealt her ran deep.

The brown envelope had been opened quickly as it had fallen onto the door mat. It had no name on it, only an address. A boring brown envelope, whose outward appearance gave no indication of its devastating contents. Over their 25 years of marriage there had been times when she had suspected his infidelity but to have this photograph, however grainy and blurred showing him naked, writhing on the two young women with the words. "Your husband" scrawled in red felt pen across it, was too much to bear. After 25 years, the feelings of betrayal and deceit were devastating. She had loved him so much.

The pain of humiliation and loss was unbearable. She knew that she had put on weight over the years, but her figure was still attractive, more rounded than in the early years of her marriage but she hadn't let herself go, her long glossy hair was shorter and more sensibly cut, her face partially hidden behind thick lensed glasses because of an inherited eye condition; but hadn't she always done her best to look good? Wasn't she always supportive and caring? Hadn't she always worked hard to enable them to have a good standard of living? How dare he humiliate her like this? All his words of kindness and love meant nothing, he was laughing at her, deceiving her, taking her for a fool. She could divorce him, but divorce was always so messy. No, she would stick with him, she wasn't giving up her comfortable life, her home, her security. No, magic was by far the most satisfactory option, she had heard about others who had used it so why not her?

*****

It was a dull Friday afternoon when Mrs Butler accessed our website. I could see her through her web camera, a not unattractive woman, mid-fifties. She looked nervous but determined. We were getting more and more enquiries from women in her age group. The dark web was opening a whole new world for them, where fantasies played out in the imagination about revenge, or to act as a deterrent to others were now a possibility. Customers could browse our site, choose an option best for them and their circumstances, place this in their shopping trolley and wait for us to deliver it to the recipient.

I typed onto her screen "Would you like to speak to a customer advisor?"

"Yes" came the reply.

"How may I help you?" I responded.

Once she had started to type, the words spread quickly across my screen flowing from this woman's anger. The hatred, the betrayal, the pain, the bitterness jumping out of every letter.

I typed back "Yes, but, how can I help you?"

After a pause the word REVENGE appeared in capital letters across my screen.

"I want him to feel my pain, the pain of someone who has loved their partner for half a lifetime and now feels that they have lost them. I want him to experience the sick feeling in his stomach, that I am feeling, the anger, the misery, the hopelessness."

As her fingers hit the keyboard I looked into her eyes, the hurt was eating away at her, the pain she was in was unbearable. I looked forward to looking into her husband's heart to see the best way to enact revenge on him. I replied that we certainly could help her to make her cheating husband feel all these things. I explained the T's and C's and that cancelation of orders was not acceptable and all orders would be fulfilled within 24 hours. She completed the transaction, paid the account and left the site.

*****

At 7.00 am the following morning, Mr Butler got out of bed and made his way downstairs to make the morning cups of tea. He glanced at the opened brown envelope on the hall table. There was no name on the envelope and once again the postman had delivered it to the wrong address. He turned it over, the edge had been unsealed, so he went to the kitchen drawer, placed some sticky tape along it and put it back on the table ready to drop through the neighbours' letterbox when he popped out later. Poor Susan he thought, her eyesight really was deteriorating, she had probably opened the letter by accident thinking it was for them. He loved her so much and hated to see her struggling. He had been thinking of retirement for a while and had been working extra hours to try to save for it, financially things would be a bit tight, but he'd be able to spend more time with her before her eyesight became too much of a disability. He would discuss it with her this morning. He shuffled back upstairs and placed the two cups of tea on his bedside table. He reached over and nudged her to wake her up; her body didn't feel right, stiff and tense. He called her name but there was no response. He scrambled over to the other side of the bed. Her body was lifeless and her skin cold, her eyes stared emptily at the ceiling. She was dead. The woman that he loved more than anything in the world was dead. The only woman that he had always remained faithful to and who had got him to put the womanizing ways of his youth behind him, was dead. His soulmate was dead. The pain was unbearable, it wrenched his stomach, and tore into his very soul, he shook violently and sobbed as his heart was torn apart. There was nothing else on earth that could have hurt him as much as this.

The screen on Mrs Butler's laptop flashed. *Your order has been completed and delivery has taken place.*

Maud

Brenda Shrewsbury

The first time it happened she was lying sated, tangled in the sheet, her head on his bare chest, watching the lights refracted in the crystal goblet that contained the last of his best scotch, as that too rested on his chest. The huge bed faced the window, a large sash Victorian bay, it was open a little, a light breeze had just wafted the muslin that covered the lower half of the original old, very thin glass.

"That breeze has a smile," she giggled. Had she really said that out loud? Then there was a slithering, swooshing sound as the books, stacked, as it turned out not so securely on the mantel shelf, slipped to the floor.

"Oh bloody hell Maud, not now" muttered Darius as he unwound his long pale legs from hers and, careless of both their modesty threw the sheet back and his body into an upright position. Confused and just a tiny bit hurt, Polly, more shrill then she meant to sound, demanded to know "who on earth is Maud?" Darius Lightfoot true to his name was already nimbly picking up the books. Turning to her with his best sardonic poet's smile Darius enquired of her "Jealous, my dear Poll?" Attempting a sophisticated "harrumph" that came more as an inexperienced squawk, nineteen year old Polly tried and failed to display an indifferent interest. "Living here my sweet you will have to get used to Maud. I promise she's no threat to you as long as you are respectful of her feelings!"

'Respectful, my arse' thought Polly, affecting what she hoped was a weary, indifferent, woman of the world look. The look (which she had been practicing in front of the old mirror in the tiny hallway) consisted of raising one eyebrow and rolling her eyes. Indifference; it was a state she had been trying to perfect since she had fallen in with the rather wonderful Darius. It would not do for him to realise just how smitten with him she was. His ego was large enough already. Just what he had seen in her three short months ago when they had met at that ludicrously pretentious literary party in Northfields, she was at a loss to know. She a nineteen year old from deepest Somerset attacking her first job as a residential social worker in a children's home for Ealing Social Services; he a thirty something part-time poet, sometime actor and, when the muse and extra's work dried up, a care assistant in an older persons care home.

Polly was having trouble processing just how she came to be here in this wonderful room in this incredible house in the most exciting city in the world. She had come to London, not to seek her fortune, she knew that as a social worker she would never be earning a fortune, but even getting a foot in the door in her West Country home town had been impossible. So London and a trainee post in a children's home it was. She hoped in these glory days of the earlier 1970s that the London Borough of Ealing would pay for her social work training, after she had paid her dues of course, working in residential care.

"So who is Maud?" she asked again.

"Resident ghost" was the muffled response from Darius. Muffled because he was now busy ferreting beneath furniture to retrieve their clothes which had been wantonly discarded all over the flat a couple of hours ago. Flat was rather a grand name for the one and a half rooms with a portion of the upstairs landing of 178 Twyford Avenue, Ealing Common. West Acton really, even then the area had pretentions but who could tell then that by the 1990s, 178 would be selling for several million pounds. Polly was shortly to take over the rental from Darius, he being off to Hollywood to make it big in the movies or to write a block buster of a screenplay! Trying and failing not to sound alarmed and incredulous Polly stated "A Ghost!" With that the wardrobe door swung open and Polly shrieked.

"Oh, no, no, no" pleaded Darius "Do not on any account show her you are frightened. She'll make your life a misery if you do." In one fluid movement he slammed the wardrobe door closed and threw Polly's clothes at her "Do you want to join me in a bath?" Despite her concern Polly smiled at the thought of lifting the work top in the tiny kitchenette to expose the large Victorian claw footed bath tub beneath, filling it with hot fragrant, steamy water and sliding in with Darius." Take that wanton look of your face you hussy," smiled Darius. At that the sash window fell down with a violent bang. A shocked Polly asked "What just happened?" Darius, tying an ancient silk dressing gown at his waist and shoving his feet into leather slippers, explained that Maud would be objecting to his use of the words wanton and hussy. "That's the trouble with living with a Victorian prude" He shouted and again the books on the mantel slithered to the floor.

Polly could hardly believe that he had been gone for nearly six months. She tried not to mind, after all this is where she wanted to be. This was the life she had planned. Independent girl about town, demanding work, (actually excruciatingly hard, soul destroying work at times). London for her to discover from Camden Lock to the V&A and all points in-between. And all the time she tried not to listen to the voice in her head asking what Darius would have thought, felt or said. As for the flat, she had loved everything about it the first time she stepped in to it. The quirky neighbours and the rather mysterious Polish landlady; Darius had claimed she was a Countess from Poland, who had fled to Ealing with her fighter pilot husband at the start of WW2. He, along with many other Polish pilots, had perished in the war. The "Countess" had been forced to take in paying guests and eventually in the 1960s had the house subdivided into half a dozen quirky flatlets cum bedsits. The Countess lived in the basement and was only ever to be seen on rent due days.

Polly knew she was lucky with the flat, a mere seventeen pounds a month and her own kitchenette and bathroom. Well, kitchenette cum bathroom. The novelty of lifting the work top to have a bath was beginning to wear off. As was trying to cook on the temperamental Baby Belling and one gas ring and as for the only source of heat in the entire flat, the hissing and popping gas fire, well she did not want to think just how noxious the fumes it gave off were. And then there was Maud!

Polly, clutching her post in her hand, climbed the once grand staircase to her front door, taking a deep breath; she inserted the key in the lock and pushed at the door. Nothing. It did not budge. Polly exhaled, willed herself to be strong and pushed again, was that a giggle she heard? The door flew open and Polly all but fell into her flat, the rucked up hall runner bunched at the back of the door. Polly knew it had been flat and lying some distance from the door when she had left that morning, just as she knew that the mirror in the tiny hall had not been turned to the wall.

Suddenly Polly had had enough, it had been a terrible day with the kids at the home running her and the other young staff ragged. And the meagre post in her hand confirmed yet again that there was no letter from Darius. Gathering her courage and giving reign to her temper Polly marched into the bedsitting room. Immediately she was struck by how cold it was, like walking into a butcher's cold room, the lower sash of the window was open as high as it could go, the curtains billowing, wardrobe door swinging wide and the books from the mantel shelf were once again on the floor. Slamming the window shut, Polly stood in the middle of the room and demanded to know of Maud "Just what are you playing at! What do you want of me, Maud?" Feeling a cold breath on the back of her neck Polly spun round but of course there was nothing there. Bursting into tears Polly sank onto the end of the bed.

Polly cried for hours. She cried because she was cold, because she was tired, because residential work was no picnic and she really wasn't sure she liked children anymore, she cried because she was home-sick and because she was tired of Maud's tricks, day after day. Mostly she cried because she missed Darius with all her heart and soul. Slowly, as she got to the hiccupping and drowning in her own snot stage, Polly realised that she was no longer cold. The bedside light was on, casting a warm glow into the room and there was the comforting hiss and pop of the ancient gas fire. She scrubbed at her swollen eyes and realised all the books were back on the mantel shelf and the wardrobe door was firmly closed. Sitting upright, Polly looked round her lovely bedsitting room and in a quavering voice asked Maud "Truce Maud? It's just you and me now; he's not coming back".

And she thought just for a second or two that there was a warm breeze with a smile on its lips in the room.

Wall

Barriers

Elizabeth Lawrence

Two people, man and woman; married for twenty five years and occupying the same living room. The wall of silence was palpable and insurmountable. Back in the family home, with its memories and comforting familiarity, knowing it was no longer his and railing against his self-destruction; she faced his deceit, betrayal and emotional abuse – all the broken dreams and promises from her one true love. He couldn't face the guilt, regret and debased lifestyle his actions had reduced him to.

Frustrated by claustrophobia and tension, he reacted, as usual, with aggression. Seeing the woman he had lost, never again to greet him with her wide, radiant smile, loving him with all her heart, trust and passion. Like the child he still was, he frequently lashed out in temper, blaming and accusing in a weak attempt to exonerate himself.

The wall could never be climbed or demolished; it was built high and strong for her self-protection, dignity and courage. And, all the while, her heart beat with the energy his physical presence always gave her.

The silence was broken from the kitchen, as his mother-in-law sang one of her many songs, with soulful resonance, 'Solitaire' - "There was a man, a lonely man, who lost his love through his indifference."

The Return

Elizabeth Lawrence

Nearing the end of her days, and more drawn than ever to the sea, she walked the shoreline, resting at times on sandy banks and upturned boats, always watching the swell of waves, enjoying each crest and break as a soothing sigh of relief and a letting go, requiring no effort.

The sea was in her blood and her life force, and always seemed to have matched the ebb and flow of her energy, turmoil, passions and peace, speaking to the depths of her soul, and connecting her to a greater spirit.

She knew this was the end – no more waves left to generate; her tide was rapidly receding. As she sat on the beach, a towering wall of water loomed over her, relentless in its power and speed, making running or screaming futile.

She faced her inevitable majestic death and the destiny she had always known, as the wall of water engulfed and claimed her.

The Wall

Louise Pople

It was 1970 when we moved to Gable End. Dad had got a job working for a local landowner as his agricultural engineer and was responsible for keeping the machinery and farm equipment running smoothly.

Dad didn't really want to move to the North but work down south was patchy, and when mum's brother found him a job in Northumberland, it seemed that the only answer to the financial hardship that Mum said we were going through was to move up North. Dad wasn't ever happy about the move, it was made from necessity but the longer the time from us replanting our roots up North, the unhappier he became.

Nothing seemed right, the house was too big, too cold and damp, the garden too large, his work too hard, the weather too wet, Mum too nagging and me too noisy. Dad changed, he got loud and angry, and frightened me when he was angry. I kept out of the way a lot. Uncle Jeff said that dad talked with his fists, I couldn't work out what this meant but as I grew older I got to know exactly what he meant, and he was right, he did talk with his fists.

I spent a lot of time in the garden of Gable End, keeping out of the way. It was a big garden and right at the end behind the wood-pile there was a wall. Not very special you might think, but this wall was special, it was very special, it was a Roman wall.

When Mr Wintersgill, who we rented the house from, showed us around the place, he made a special point of showing us the wall and telling us all about its history. The wall was about 12 feet long and 6 feet high and was built at about the same time as Emperor Hadrian's wall. Mr Wintersgill had some documents from English Heritage that confirmed everything that he told us, and that the wall was probably part of a small town surrounding a fort about a mile away.

There was also a list of rules to do with the wall that we had to abide by. We weren't allowed to touch it or even go near it. In fact, there was a gravelled area about 3 feet out from the wall which we weren't allowed to set foot inside. We were to visually inspect the wall once a month, reporting any damage, and allow English Heritage access to it every 6 months for an inspection.

I loved the wall, I couldn't believe that it could be so old, and I felt important that we were the guardians of it. Because dad was not himself, as Mum would say, I spent a lot of time keeping out of the way, sitting crossed legged on the grass, staring at the wall. I wondered who had built it, why it had been built and what the people were like who lived where our house was over 2 thousand years ago. I was fascinated by the shape of its stones and the channels that the rain had made between them allowing it to find its way down to the soil. On the wall about half way up was a large stone tile with a carved lions head on it. It really was a wonderful work of art. I spent hours sketching the wall and the lion, taking photographs on my Polaroid camera and making up stories about the Romans who had built it.

By 1975 we had lived in the house for five years. Dad hated it; he hated the house, hated his job, hated Mum for making him move up North, hated Mum's brother, Jeff, and hated me. I became good at keeping out of the way, but Mum couldn't do this as well as me, but she did become good at lying. Oh, how she laughed with Mrs Roberts my class teacher as she made up a comic scene of her tripping over her slippers, kicking the cat and then knocking her head on the mantelpiece as she tumbled to the floor. Lie number one, she never wore slippers, lie number two we didn't have a cat. I don't know what kind of talk Dad was having with mum with his fists, but it must have been colourful, to paint her face in so many shades of black and blue.

On 30th March 1975 Mum had had enough of Dad's fist talking and whilst I was at school, walked through the back door down through the garden and out of our lives. Dad said that she needed her freedom and was going off to find a job in a holiday camp on the East coast. I knew Mum wouldn't leave without me, I was her best girl and I looked after her. I waited for her to write, to send me a ticket to the holiday camp, but it didn't arrive so, wherever she had gone, she'd gone without me. One thing I couldn't understand was how she could have got to the East coast in only one shoe as I found one of her best red sling backs in the garden down by the wall the next day. I searched through her wardrobe but the other one was nowhere to be seen. I had seen her wearing them the day before so how could she have got to the East Coast in one shoe? I took her other shoe and wrapped it in tissue paper from her dress drawer, held it close to my chest and then hid it inside a shoebox under my bed. I don't know why I didn't ask Dad about it, but I didn't.

Dad said we didn't need Mum as she was useless anyway and didn't love us and now I would have to grow up pretty damn fast as he couldn't do all the housework and cooking. It was a shame his new best friend Jack Daniels couldn't help us out. Dad spent so long with him these days, muttering into his whiskey glass about who he could have been, where he could be today if he hadn't married the useless bitch. Jack listened patiently to his tales of woe, sometimes calming him and sending him off to sleep in the armchair and sometimes winding him up to shout and swear and stumble around the place. At times like this the cupboard under the stairs was my out of the way place. My friend Henry the Hoover was far more benevolent company than Dad's friend Jack.

I didn't get down to the wall much, once Mum had gone, and, like Mum, I wasn't able to keep out of the way as much either. When I did go down to the wall it wasn't the same any more. The wall stood there as it always had for two thousand years but the area around it had changed. The grassed area where I usually sat was bumpier than usual and muddier than usual. Dad told me to stop wasting my time there or he would tell English heritage that he had seen me damaging the wall. I hadn't of course, although I do admit to reaching up and stroking the lion's face on the plaque, something stable in my very unstable life.

The following autumn, after mum had left, the English heritage lady made her twice yearly visit to inspect the wall. Dad was uneasy about her visit, "stupid bitch, bloody waste of time!" but he took her down to the wall and stood with her whilst she did the inspection. He told me I had to wait in the house and not speak to "the heritage bitch" otherwise I'd get a backhander. When the heritage bitch had left, Dad seemed more agitated than ever. It seemed she had put in her report that the area around the wall was disturbed and wanted another check made to ensure that the foundations of the wall hadn't been damaged.

Dad was fuming. I talked to his fist a couple of times and then he sat in his well-worn armchair next to the empty fireplace to have a good long chat with Jack, who listened attentively to his mitherings until the early hours of the morning. I made up a bed under the stairs as I knew that he would be too drunk to manage the locks on the door and I lay there in the darkness, paralysed with fear, praying for Jack to lull him to sleep. At about 2 in the morning, things changed, Dad suddenly became loud and violent; I could hear glass smash and splinter around the room. I heard him stumble into the garden where Mum's name was shouted and cursed across the dales of Northumberland. As his voice became more distant I left my hiding place and stood in the window watching him weaving his way down towards the wall. I followed at a distance, feeling grateful for my soft fluffy slippers carrying me silently over the lawn, through the orchard to a spot behind the woodpile where I could see him silhouetted in the moonlight.

He dropped to his knees and started digging in the area where I had sat for so many years gazing at the ancient stones in front of me. His hands, like large unyielding shovels, stripped away the grass and stones grabbing handfuls of earth and dropping them clumsily at his side. Soon he found what he was looking for and pulled and pulled so that the soil was forced to release its hold on a mud caked red sling back shoe.

My silence broke as my mouth opened and inhaled the cold night air and a loud rasping gasp choked up from my throat. Dad looked up and I froze as his steely eyes searched me out in the shadows. He stared straight into my horrified eyes "Stupid cow" he shouted, "what are you doing here?" "Spying on me eh? Wait till I get hold of you." I shook violently and screamed "Murderer" as he stumbled to his feet to lunge towards me, but his friend Jack had other ideas, as he took his feet from under him and toppled him backwards, smashing his head against the wall. The wall shattered with his weight and the force of his fall, and stones crushed and buried the anger in his face as he left this world taking with him 2,000 years of history.

For the first time in years I sobbed, hot tears flowing from my eyes. Tears, as the wall that I was charged with protecting lay at my feet. The English Heritage lady had said that the wall had stood through the fall of the Roman Empire and the unrest of the Anglo-Saxon era, the Vikings, the Normans, the spread of Christianity and the rise of the royal houses. It had stood firm through civil war and two world wars. It had witnessed civilization evolve and our world change beyond recognition. One thing that it didn't survive though, was my dad and his mate Jack Daniels.

After a night of blue flashing lights and visits from well-meaning neighbours that I had never met before, offering their help, I was taken to stay with a family in Morpeth. A very nice woman, Mary, helped me pack a few things and a shiny Datsun Cherry whisked me away as tents and barriers were erected around the wall and Police tapes surrounded my house.

Police officers visited me most days to talk about life at The Gables, then about two weeks after the day that my dad cheated English heritage out of one of its valued remains, I had news of my mum. It seems she had been traced to Pontins Holiday Park in Great Yarmouth where she was working behind the bar through the summer and as a cleaner out of season. She was going to be getting the train to Morpeth the following day.

After investigation it was found that Dad had buried all the love letters that she had ever written to him, along with her wedding dress, their wedding album and her best red shoes (or at least one of them) in a trench that he had dug by the wall, probably after Jack had told him to get them all out of the house one evening. Maybe he couldn't bear to have these memories of happier times around him anymore. I just felt so very sad. I loved that wall.

Menu

Best Friends Forever?

Fenja Hill

The first time I saw a menu, I was fifteen years old. Until then, the only time I had eaten out was in a department store cafeteria, where, at that time, there was no menu. You could buy tea (none of your fancy flavours – British rail standard was good enough for everyone in those days) and coffee (if you had ideas above your station) and a limited selection of cold drinks, and there would be cake and sandwiches, but everything was on open display and there was no need to create a list from which customers might select their snack. My mother would have a cup of tea, and my sisters and I would have orange squash and on a good day we might also have a doughnut.

As a teenager I was sent to boarding school, so that the constant relocations of the family wouldn't disrupt my GCEs. Occasionally, on a Sunday, parents were allowed to come and take us out for a few hours and, on this particular day, as mine were in Germany, I was invited to spend the day with a friend and her parents.

I had never met Chris's parents before, so there was a degree of natural discomfort. She was a good friend but parents were a whole other thing. Having friends at boarding school wasn't the same as having them where you lived, because you never saw them in their home environment or with other family members; you didn't get used to seeing their mum when you went to call for them or to sitting in their room and playing records, which was what I did in the holidays, or seeing their dad when he came in from work and everyone turned their sound levels down a notch and the younger children stopped torturing each other.

They had a very nice car but all I remember is desperately hoping we weren't going far, because I used to get horribly car-sick and if I had thrown up in their car I would have been mortified. Fortunately, it wasn't far and anyway I felt fine. It was many, many years before I understood that my childhood car-sickness was caused by the fact that my parents chain-smoked throughout every journey.

Chris's parents were not smokers, so my fears were not realised, but I still recall the tension. Also, they hadn't thought to say where we were going or what plans they had for the day. Looking back, they had probably mentioned it to Chris but she would have assumed I'd be fine and hadn't bothered to pass that information on.

It's probably just as well I didn't know, because my anxiety levels would have rocketed. The car was parked, and we crossed the road and headed into a restaurant. At that point, I would have gladly run off into the distance. To my inexperienced eyes, it looked really posh although, thinking back, it was probably a very average place. More than a Wimpy but a long way from Michelin Star.

We sat down and I watched every move that they made, and also the people around us. Suddenly, in spite of Chris being my best friend and her parents so far having been very nice to me, I was terrified of embarrassing myself. I somehow understood that there was more at stake here. They were all, including Chris, completely comfortable with the environment, perusing their menus, talking to waiters, chatting with one another, whereas I had just been dumped on an alien planet and I knew that my parents too would have struggled. My first experience of class as an issue.

My father was working class. Before he joined the RAF he was a skilled bricklayer and, after he joined, he never progressed beyond the rank of Corporal. Neither of my parents were educated beyond the age of fourteen – something my mother constantly regretted because she was an intelligent woman, convinced that she could have done much more with her life, living in a permanent state of disappointment.

God only knew what Chris's dad did before joining the RAF, but it was probably nothing. I imagine he went straight into military training from school, or possibly university, and came out as an officer. For the first time, I saw the huge gulf between myself and Chris, invisible when sitting in a classroom, or curled up in the common-room in our pyjamas watching Top of the Pops.

I have no idea what I ate that day. I know that I watched and listened as though my life depended on it. Apart from anything else, I could see the prices on the menu and they seemed so high that I was terrified. How could I expect people I had never met before to pay that kind of money for my dinner? (This was many years before I learned to call my midday meal lunch).

I clutched the menu and tried to choose something from what seemed like an amazing selection of foods. To be honest, I have a vague recollection of omelettes being one of the options, but I can remember nothing else. I must have ordered something – probably whatever Chris was having. I know I wanted to ask for water to drink because it was surely cheaper than all the juices and things on the menu, but I couldn't see it on there anywhere so, in the end, I had a coke, like Chris.

I ate carefully and politely, and tried to join in the conversation when a question was directed at me, without speaking with my mouth full. Nobody laughed and pointed and my relationship with Chris remained the same afterwards, so I must have carried it off.

Chris's dad stole a piece of food from Chris's plate and I learned from the ensuing good-natured banter that this was not good manners and not something you should do when eating outside your own home, or even *at* home, if there was company. Was I company?

The biggest thing I learned that day though, was that Chris and I, best friends for two years, would not be friends when we left school. I learned that, outside the cocoon of the classroom and the boarding house, we lived in different universes. Chris had never shared a bedroom until she went to boarding school. I had never slept alone. Chris didn't have pocket money, she had an allowance. Her family went abroad every year for their holidays and, although they lived in RAF accommodation wherever her father was posted to, they owned a house in Lincoln, that was their own and that they lived in whenever it was practical. It had four bedrooms and two bathrooms.

There was a stream running across the bottom of the garden. One of the ponies in the field across the road was Chris's but it was looked after for her by a local family. Chris and her family ate out regularly, they drove up to London and stayed in hotels to go shopping. They were the perfect Enid Blyton family, and I had never known, because boarding school, with its regimen, its uniform, its standard food and timetables, was an equaliser so powerful that neither of us had ever glimpsed the reality of one another's lives in the outside world.

Chris's dad wrote on the menu – they were having some kind of discussion and he wanted to remind himself of something. I was horrified and convinced that we would be thrown out, but the waiter just handed the menu to me, as the closest person to him, and said I could take it as a souvenir of our day out. I held it to me all the way back to school in the car and as soon as I was alone, I took it round the back by the kitchen doors and buried it in a bin full of food waste.

Language Enrichment

Elizabeth Lawrence

The Prologue

One of the highlights of this year was a writers' retreat in Lyme Regis. The four of us who were lucky enough to go had chosen Lyme after reading Remarkable Creatures, and loving the descriptions of the sea and quaint cottages. With the added possibility of finding fossils on the beach, we set off with great enthusiasm and optimism. We agreed that we had the high levels of excited expectation of children on Christmas Eve! A spring holiday in tranquillity and sunshine after a long winter was very appealing; and Cobb Cottage with its sea views and sun terrace seemed perfect.

I travelled with Fenja in her car, and there was real concern about the amount of luggage I needed, to cover all potential disasters, including Tsunami and famine. With much good humour, I was well accommodated, and Macaque took the excess in his car with Lois. The journey was the start of us all getting to know each better in the spirit of a shared adventure; and the spring sunshine, floral hedgerows and quiet roads marked a lovely beginning.

As we approached the tranquil haven of Lyme, a dreamlike quality unfolded and remained for the duration of our stay; as if the beautiful coastal town had been awaiting our arrival and put on its best sunshine, floral display and empty streets to stroll and explore at leisure.

Once we had gained access to the cottage using every expletive in the English Language, old and new, in an attempt to unlock the door and finally resorted to climbing through a window, we luxuriated into four days of easy, stimulating company. Endless book shops with cosy open fires and jazz music, cafes and gentle walks along the coast in sunshine, or by moonlight, was heaven to us all. We seemed to laugh our way through the days, as individual idiosyncrasies emerged with great hilarity; and then the constant challenge of trying to work a high tech kitchen in order to produce the simplest of meals – but good company, wine and music can solve anything.

One of the highlights was Macaque's poetry workshop, imparting his love and joy of poetry and a few tips and techniques to help us on our way. We were greatly inspired to think poetically and have a go with our own style, having been assured 'there are no rules, just the stipulation that it must be memorable.' We had each brought our own projects to work on, and with frequent breaks, walking together by the sea, exploring the town, bookshops and cafes, it was a concentrated period of absorbing and enjoying our surroundings whilst being able to express ideas in a creative way, expanding and encouraging each other.

I was inspired, just being in a creative environment with likeminded people – and ribbed quite a lot, about 'just thinking about writing', but not actually doing it! Fair and true comment, but writers tuck away ideas for future use - a friend said I percolate mine, like coffee - and we had many an excellent brew in our cosy cottage! '!

The four days away formed a bond between us, and we are now 'the Lyme Four', continuing to find adventures, such as a trip to Caerphilly Castle this autumn, in search of dragons. One of us recently made the comment, "how lucky we are to have found each other – we're like the Famous Five!" We are thinking about a dog to make five! But we are a writing group of eleven, and still growing, so who knows what adventures lie ahead in 2019; and the more the merrier!

And so, with this month's '"Menu" writing assignment, my thoughts turned to Lyme and seagulls, which were the bane of our time there.

Main Course

Aha! Newcomers in town! Word had spread on the air waves that a writing group, enchanted by Lyme and ready to dream their way through the next few days, would shortly be strolling, unaware, along the quay. Sure enough, the happy group took their ease, enraptured by the spring sunshine, blue sea and olde-worlde charm of the promenade. The first attack was a cinch on such a relaxed, trusting and unguarded group. Soup and a bread roll on the menu today – a speedy descent, a quick tap on the back of the head with beak closed, wings expanded to confuse and blind fold, and off with the bread roll, showering a full bowl of soup onto as much clothing as possible, creating havoc and ensuring a quick getaway. The shouts of "Oi!" and "Fuck off!" only added to our victory roll as I took off with my trophy. Although, we had our doubts as to whether they really were writers, given their use of language. Safely out of vision, and bread roll satisfyingly gulped, we eyed the group, mopping each other and warning others – it may not be so easy next time.

Dessert

The second attack always takes more precision and sniper-like expertise. Two writers down and two to go, we spotted an easy target; with an ice cream held invitingly high, to reveal my favourite flavour – mmmm, black cherry!

As both heads turned naturally, to admire the sun on the sea, I swooped with lightning speed and snatched the cone, luckily, hardly even licked by the unsuspecting victim. Again, as I soared out of range, devouring fresh deliciousness, even louder this time, "Fuck off!!", and "Fucking seagulls!!" rang, loudly in my ears. The writers were definitely warming up!

Footnote and disclaimer

Unknown to us all, Lois was logging all of our hilarious incidents and remarks and compiled a highly amusing booklet, presenting us each with a copy when we got home. I have yet to read it without collapsing into helpless laughter!

Full names have been withheld to protect the magnificent. The company was gloriously stimulating and inspiring, with great use of language and sharing of ideas. I learned how to put Anglo Saxon words to good use, in a descriptive context; and now fully understand the saying, "A brilliant mind and a foul mouth is a formidable combination!"

Menu

Macaque

The men you look for
The men you want
The men who want you
The men you fall for
The men you take home
The men who take you

The men you cry for
The men who make you

The men you chat to
Take back to your flat to
Have coffee and more
The men you meet who
Only mistreat you
And call you a whore

The men you cook for
Do yourself up for
Buy new clothes for
Put yourself out for
The men you pout for

The men you dance for
Who offer romance for
A week or two
The men who forsake you
Repeatedly break you
The men you turn to
The men you choose

They're not fucking worth it

Driftwood

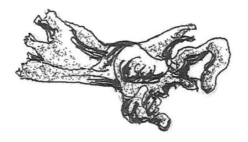

Jetsam Coming Home

Jane Barron

He lived in a large room of the old house, anonymous and happy for that. He had found the driftwood on the early morning beach as the tide crept away, like the cloaking darkness of the night. He brought it home, struggling with the length and awkwardness of the shape, but with a sense of purpose and anticipation that belied his shuffling and stumbling gait. In his room he surveyed his space with an artist's eye.

He remembered gleefully an old device originally used for gripping sheets of wood together while the glue set, and found the object, jumbled in among the detritus he brought back to his room, freed from charity shops, the street, bins and the beach.

It was aged and heavy, rusted, and hard to open its jaws, but he finally managed it with help from some WD40 and, with satisfaction, moved on to his next step. He perused today's find, with a knowing nod to the odds and ends heaped in the corner of the room. His treasures, obscure, unwanted and sometimes damaged items that somehow he found beautiful. He had carried each of them home with the same excitement warming in his chest, anticipating a moment of awakening like this.

He shuddered momentarily, the memory suddenly vivid, of his past creations, taken out of his control for the world to applaud. Then that same world, to overwhelm him with the demand for more and more, like a prowling beast. He slowed his breathing and calmed his heart as he had been taught, he came back slowly into the darkened room that was now his home.

Addressing now, the long length of the gnarled and twisted wood, he ran his hand along the wave-washed smoothness of the curve and then the rough texture where it splayed out into a myriad of tiny empty shoots. Examining the minute detail of each twist and knot he whispered to the wood, "Beautiful, you are just beautiful."

He opened the device as wide as possible and pushed it onto the edge of the old plaster mantelshelf. He manoeuvred the wood until he could grip it firmly against the mantel, allowing the curve to sweep up to the high ceiling while the rest of the at least eight foot length, curled slightly outward and downward into the room, with the spreading shoots like a collection of tiny gun barrels. He tightened the device, then, standing back, he sighed with a gentle pleasure. It spoke to him of oceans, white beaches like aprons around lush islands of palm trees. It sang of the winds and high waves that crashed and dipped under a huge sky. Now, suspended and still, the soft colour tones of the wood flickered in candlelight, because despite the early morning light as he returned from the beach, he never opened the curtains – he sheltered here, this was his own world where he kept his fragile mind safe.

In another life, he had been discovered as an original artist seemingly with a future of wonderful possibilities. But he could not endure the endless invasion into the meaning and purpose of his work and his solitary nature rebelled, his mind bewildered. He had sunk into a pit of anxiety and despair, hounded into becoming insular and reclusive.

Bereft of all that he had been before, now he ventured out rarely, and only to search for the little nuggets of treasure that gave him hope, scurrying back to his bedsit to enjoy them in his own inviolable world. The lovely house he had owned was sold and he was now living on benefits, the money all gone, and his interaction with the real world minimal. But he found that inside this house, this home, at last he had been able to slowly abandon his fear and finally, to create for himself alone. He gazed at the driftwood placed perfectly and his heart sang with joy.

Beach Treasures

Elizabeth Lawrence

The very name has always sent my imagination soaring. Driftwood - solid, and yet, washed randomly onto shores around the world with sea wrack. How far does it travel and on what tides and currents? Sometimes planed by beatings against rocks and shingles to rounded, curved and soft edges, or smoothed and flattened, pleasingly bleached by sun and salt until clean and stark. As children, we brought driftwood home from the beach and claimed the pieces as our own. The house name was painted onto driftwood, in my dad's shaky hand with gloss paint and a child's paintbrush – but the pride in our homemade name plate was immense!

Beach combing was a natural part of our lives, regularly returning home, trailing strands of seaweed with huge root balls, shells, and pieces of driftwood. I often wondered about the wood, stroking its smooth surface – imagining shipwrecks or furniture washed away by flood, and a once loved and prized possession; part of the ageing process, and yet, retaining a use, value and beauty; a relic – a survivor, changed but still here!

We could always rely on finding driftwood for decorating sand sculptures, a broomstick or a paddle for an air bed; and always with a dog, jumping excitedly waiting for a stick to be thrown – and sometimes being allowed to carry the prized wood in his mouth.

A flower bed in the garden always seemed more enchanting when decorated with driftwood borders and seashells. My grandmother used to take shells home for her garden in the industrial north east; which always made me feel sad.

With driftwood in the home we can escape to salty air, sun-bleached sand, simplicity and the elements. The irregular shapes, unvarnished, in contrast to the usual neat, ordered lines in domestic use. Driftwood's appeal is its wildness; as if still a living thing brought to life by the ravages of the ocean, aesthetically pleasing in its unfinished state.

I share a fear with many, of one day being housebound. I would need to be surrounded by as much of the natural world as possible.

A large wall-mounted piece of driftwood, such as the one at The Bay, where my writing group meets, would bring enormous comfort, providing memories of silky warm sand, upturned wooden boats and the roar of the ocean.

If I Drift

Fenja Hill

If I drift, would you
throw me a line,
catch my hand,
anchor me?

If I drift, would you
seduce me
with your siren song,
back to your waiting arms?

or

If I drift, would you
float,
relaxing on the waves,
certain, the next tide
will bring me home.

Time

Time-slip

Jane Barron

In the Time Factory, Mr Jarvis, the manager, busied himself today with the accounting figures. A respected but pernickety boss, he would quip "Time is time!" as he did his rounds on the factory floor, or "Marking time again Higgins?" His staff smiled indulgently and continued their labours in the calm atmosphere of inevitability. Time was rolled up and on in their expert celestial hands.

During this normally unhurried morning, the factory floor became alarmingly subdued and the whirring slowed considerably. Jarvis looked up, and leaned over the open mezzanine level overlooking the factory floor. His desk was placed conveniently close to the wrought iron railings, fashioned in glorious Fleur de Lys, that bordered the edge of the mezzanine floor.

The foreman stood awkwardly gazing up at him, then nervously picked up the inter-factory phone, indicating rather pointlessly, Jarvis thought, to the instrument before placing it by his ear. Jarvis raised his receiver and listened for a moment before shooting suddenly upright from his chair, and barking into the phone.

"What do you mean you lost some time? A minute? A day?" His whole body went stiff as he repeated, "You lost 1953... and 1974!!! Deleted? Did you lose the hard copy too?" He waved his arms above the floor of workers who were now floundering about below, checking machines and getting very agitated. "Look for them people!" he cried.

Listening again to the phone, he watched his foreman stare at the tumbling numbers on the screen of his large machine then turn to look up at him, a look of sheer terror on his face and spoke shakily to his manager.

"The years are backing up.... and 2001 is fading?" Jarvis repeated. "Fading? Fading away completely?" he asked, stunned. "This can't be happening – it's impossible, it's impossible!"

Lurching from his desk, Jarvis, hands on head in disbelief and panic, visibly steadied himself, and turning to his administrator, took a deep breath. "Brenda, call the Boss." She reached for the red phone but he rushed forward and grasped it from her. "No, no – hold on a minute, think, think man!" He paced up and down for a couple of minutes, shaking his head and muttering to himself, but stopped again in front of her, his shoulders drooped and he repeated the original command. "Yes, we need to call the Boss right now."

A shriek from the works floor brought him back to the phone in a sweat, "What? What?" he shouted into the mouthpiece. He listened and turned pale, "All of BC is gone!?"

Leaning over the balcony, he adopted a loud, authoritative, if somewhat shaky voice to instruct everyone. "Calm yourselves, people, calm yourselves – now tell me who was last to leave last night?" The workforce stared up at him frozen with fear. "Well?" No mistaking, this was a screech!

Fingers pointed to a young man, cowering behind a machine and pressed him forward. "Get him here. Now!" Jarvis was apoplectic but fighting hard to maintain a modicum of control over his flailing arms and contorted features.

The trembling man stood pressed against the foreman who held his arm firmly to make sure he was going nowhere.

"Stand there," ordered Jarvis. "What did you do as you left last night? Remember man, think, think!" The young man mumbled into his handkerchief and was beginning to snivel.

Cocking his head closer, Jarvis exclaimed, "The Red Button, did you say red button? The man nodded and shrank back against the foreman.

"The Red Button, the Red Button that no one is supposed to ever touch, including me?" As the man stammered his explanation, Jarvis repeated it shouting out each sentence, stamping about and flailing his arms at no one in particular.

"You might have brushed it with your finger? No, your hand? Maybe your arm? You fell against it and it went off," he was screaming now. Clasping his forehead, he leaned against the wall. "I can't speak.....get me a chair......It went off and nothing happened so you just went home..?" This he repeated almost to himself, incredulous.

"TIME IS RUNNING DOWN THE DRAIN OF OBLIVION! That's what's happening!" he cried, poking the poor broken man in the chest with each word. He stood, momentarily spent, only to become aware that a voice was shouting his name.

"WHAT?" he spun round to face Brenda who had been trying to get a word in between outbursts.

"The Boss said what? What date?" he barked bemused. "Have we checked today's date? Did you tell him about the chaos going on down here Brenda?"

Glancing condescendingly about him, Jarvis calmly enquired if anyone knew.

"Today's bloody date, anyone?"

"Monday the what? Louder", he admonished his administrator, his face towered above hers.

And bracing herself, she declared, "Today is Monday, the 1st of April!"

This was followed by a deafening silence, the whole factory had been standing in frozen panic and listened to every word over the factory intercom. Jarvis had inadvertently pressed the switch in his fury, while clutching the phone. They all absorbed this information as if in a vacuum. No one dared move a muscle.

After a long moment, Jarvis lowered himself carefully into a chair and nodding to Brenda told her to call the boss back. "Tell him, screamingly funny. We're all having a good laugh down here too...." He slumped over the desk. "I need to lie down ...."

An Idea of Heaven

Fenja Hill

In the beginning, there was bugger all really. Just a patch of ground, covered with an assortment of rotting leaves, cigarette ends, plastic bags, condom wrappers and empty cans; and one blue glove. A couple of pieces of broken glass, shoved into a corner by the crumbling fence, in a half-hearted attempt to make it, if not safer, at least less dangerous. The metal framework of an ancient bench served no practical purpose any longer, the wooden slats of seat and back-rest were long gone. Nothing grew.

The middle bit was amazing. There were only three of us at first, but, over time, passing strangers saw what was happening and stopped to help, sometimes just for half an hour, but sometimes for the rest of the day. Some came back and some didn't, some just did what was asked, and some had suggestions, ideas for stuff we hadn't thought of. We learnt some of their names, I'm still in touch with two of them. The litter was bagged up and taken away, carefully sorted into recyclable, non-recyclable and potentially dangerous. The ground was dug over, paths were laid, topsoil was brought in, with the help of Tom's van. Tom was one of the stayers. The fence was fixed with planks of wood taken from the old decking that Sarah was replacing in the house she had just moved into. Aliyah only stopped by once, but the paintings on the fence were her idea. Lacey got into trouble with her mum because she kept getting home from school late. She just had to stop every day and help. By the second week, her mum was meeting her there with a sandwich and drink, and a pair of scruffy trousers, so she wouldn't ruin her school ones. We all stood round her in a circle, facing outwards, while she changed. That was before Keith turned up with all the parts for a tiny garden shed that took us three days to put together. After that, someone painted 'Lacey's changing room' on the door, although, of course, we did start to store tools and stuff in there too.

The planting was random. People would turn up with a plant and put it in where there was a gap. We were painters and decorators, nurses, a traffic warden, schoolchildren, shop assistants, cleaners, a plumber. We were not gardeners; there was no plan, no design. The gaps got fewer and fewer. Some of the plants flourished and some struggled, but we didn't pull any of them up. We knew that next year they would be fine.

There was so much colour, so much laughter, so much care. When all the gaps were full of plants and the path had stopped wobbling and the shed was finally steady on the paving slabs rescued from the refuse dump and the last bits of fencing had stopped threatening to collapse on the lavender, we had a party. Who knew that Alice had a guitar? Who knew that Jason and Kyle could sing like that? And who knew that Adeel could dance? People passing by stopped, not to help this time, but to enjoy our magic garden, to sing and dance with us.

The end was brutal. The door to the shed hung, splintered, from one twisted hinge. The paint we had been keeping to finish the final bits of fence mural had been used to slash words of hatred and anger across our beautiful pictures. Our tools had been used to rip the plants from their safe beds and heap them together in the centre of our garden before urinating all over them. The stink was foul. There had been a half-hearted attempt to burn them, but it had failed. Perhaps that was why they resorted to pissing on them; they didn't want us to re-plant. In spite of the failure to properly ignite, there were dark, charred leaves and, for a few moments, I believed that I could hear the flowers screaming. Glass from the smashed window of the shed had been carefully planted in the disturbed earth and then loosely covered. We didn't see this until Ellie knelt to try and rescue a plant that was still semi-rooted in the soil. Adeel took her to A&E. I haven't seen her since.

Inside the shed, nailed to the back wall, was a piece of A4 paper, torn roughly from a pad. Surprisingly neat handwriting.

Your idea of heaven is not ours.

Rhythms of Life

Elizabeth Lawrence

Your time was of summer
And endless giving
The minutes that sprang life
Have left me empty
Now my time is of another time
And the race goes on without me

Time can be bought, given, spent, enjoyed, endured, wasted, counted, but, not yet, travelled – as far as we know.

As someone who struggles with time, admonishments of "tempus fugit" or "time waits for no man" (perhaps it waits for women?) only add to a sense of trying to catch a moving train, or quickening one's natural rhythm of life; like being in the wrong gear while the engine strains and makes a jarring noise; using more fuel and causing wear and tear.

We each need to extract what we can from life; wherever our minds, memories, imaginations and drives take us; with different cruising speeds. Situations that some speed through, others may need time to linger, absorb, reflect and savour – wasting time, some may say, but this can be essential repair work, as daydreaming leads to creativity. I believe there is research to back this up – a good excuse, anyway!

Time is perhaps the greatest gift to give anyone, alongside love, and is becoming even more precious in a fast age. What satisfaction and joy, from taking time to listen, teach, care, entertain, laugh or just share space and ' be there' with another. The wonders of exploring endless time with others.

To measure time in mechanical minutes seems relentlessly structured. I wish it were measured in moment of bliss, connections with people, nature or whatever individual passions may be; a hobby where the self is forgotten and the product takes on a separate life and identity, as we lose ourselves in time.

We each have a different time span on this earth, which is measured in years, with some reaching old age, seemingly detached from relationships and humanity; whereas, others make a difference for example, through art, science, medicine etc. And some, after only a short time in years, leave a legacy for future generations, as they impart love and wisdom to comfort the bereaved for the rest of their lives. But it's the unknown and unmeasured I find so fascinating – a chance meeting, or conversation, that changes lives and events. It's often the impromptu and unstructured that lead to change and creativity. So, could time be better measured by influence, impact and enjoyment of life?

I am not so idealistic as to imagine the commercial world, infrastructure, health and education, could function without "strict time keeping" (the very phrase sends shudders down my spine!); but each to their own choosing, and it is an act of kindness to let people live by their own versions of time.

A good friend recently gave me a lovely, thoughtful gift of a clock, with the inscription "who cares, I'm late anyway" – this gives enormous comfort and cheer as I glance up, to check the time, usually late!

In the meantime, I continue racing against the clock to meet friends, as 'shared time' is indeed a precious gift.

Schrodinger's Chronometer

Macaque

Henry stood in the colonnade outside the lecture theatre, reading the notices pinned up on the various boards. His ankle-length Oxfam overcoat was unbuttoned, the collar turned up inside his curtain of loose, wavy hair, and his shabby canvas rucksack, adorned with the logos and lyrics of numerous heavy metal bands rendered in biro, hung nonchalantly by one strap over his right shoulder.

He had been there, feigning a casual interest in the notices for ten minutes, not because he was a habitually keen student or a chronically early riser, but because he knew that it took about twenty minutes to walk there from his digs. He knew very well, for example, that when he set off ten minutes before the start of a lecture, he always arrived ten minutes late, so this morning he had allowed twenty minutes for the walk, and arrived ten minutes early. He had been mulling this twist of fate over since his premature arrival, but now his vexation turned to appreciation as he noticed a poster advertising a visit by the American poet John Ashbery to a venue on the South Bank. He wondered if Elizabeth would be interested in attending it.

"Hey!" said a bright voice behind him. He turned to see Beth smiling at him over a pile of files and books. She looked stunning in the drab shade of the old stone columns, her blond hair and silver pentagram earrings seeming to glow in the morning light. "Are you walking to American Lit.?" she asked, with a half turn of her shoulders in the direction of the seminar room.

"No...erm...could you take notes for me? I'm crashing a lecture on The Philosophy of Time."

"The Philosophy of Time? Really?" Her earrings glinted with surprise.

"Yeah, I thought it might help me understand Burnt Norton, you know, '*Time present and time past are both perhaps present in time future...*'"

"*And time future contained in time past,*" she completed for him. "I just thought Eliot was being obtuse."

"Well, hopefully, I'll let you know!" he laughed.

"Ok, well, I don't want to be late. See you around, maybe," and with a shrug of her laden arms, she trotted off down the stone steps.

'Idiot!' he thought, as he watched her disappear out of sight, as the great wooden doors opened and the people around him began to funnel into the auditorium. 'Idiot! Idiot! Why didn't you mention the Ashbery thing? Perfect opportunity! Brainless idiot!'

Henry sat at the back of the auditorium and took out his notepad and pen. He often sat in on philosophy and psychology lectures during his free periods, and usually went unnoticed, but today's lecturer was unknown to him. He looked like a stocky Einstein as he took a sheaf of papers from his battered briefcase and placed them on the desk in front of the blackboard. He was of the old school, clearly: tweed jacket and checked shirt with bow tie and V-neck sweater, corduroy trousers in pale octarine, white hair, and a briefcase like a Victorian doctor's. Henry was pleased; the mad ones always gave more interesting talks.

"Right, ladies or gentlemen – it's not easy to tell these days – settle down, please!" he called in a remarkably clear voice for such an aged looking character. Henry stopped doodling pentagrams and gazed out of the high windows at the brightening blue of the morning sky. 'Why didn't I ask her about Ashbery?' he thought despairingly.

"Come on, settle down," repeated the professor. "If I had wanted to spend my employment shouting at idiots, I would have stayed in the army." Henry turned his attention back to the present.

"Thank you. Now, today, and for the next couple of weeks, we are going to be considering the nature and philosophy of time, and there will be an essay due at the end of May. Now, who can tell me what Time is?"

"It's ten past nine, sir!" said a boy in a red woollen sweater, seated in the front row. Before the ensuing laughter could take hold, however, the professor said calmly:

"Prove it."

"Uh, the clock up there says so," said the boy, with a little less bravado.

The professor stepped round the desk, gazing theatrically at the clock and back at his audience with a quizzical expression. He stopped in front of the boy in the red sweater, but addressed the whole room:

"Ten past nine…but why ten past nine? What do those numbers mean? Why the 7th of March? Why 1998? What is the *meaning*, what is the true *purpose*, what is the *nature* of time?"

The man was now speaking to a silent room. Henry excitedly made notes, beginning to formulate inadequate answers in his mind to some of these questions.

"How many of you think that time is real? Hands up."

Two thirds of the students raised their hands, the remaining third clearly representing the shy and confused as well as the sceptical.

"And how many of you believe in a Unified Space Time, a golden standard of Time, if you will?" A fluctuation in the array of raised hands. "Interesting. Right, so today we are going to examine our flawed perceptions of time; we will look at the challenges posed by Solar Time – how it is still half past eight in Cornwall, and the 6th of March in Papua New Guinea; we will be looking at a principal I like to call Schrodinger's Chronometer, and hopefully get onto Linear versus Non Linear conceptions by the end of today's lecture. Next week, I hope to cover quantum clocks and Ayurvedic Time."

Henry continued to make notes. Although his strengths undoubtedly lay in literary subjects, he was fascinated by science and philosophy, and was always invigorated by the lectures he managed to crash. He often found, however, that his comprehension of the theories that so caught his attention at the time faded when he returned to the notes he had taken, or tried to explain some element of particle physics to his flatmates. By the end of the lecture, he was thoroughly looking forward to considering the conundrum the professor had posed for the seminar he wouldn't be attending: whether a race of humanoids on a planet orbited by two glowing moons, denied any change in light or season, would develop a concept of time.

He snuck past the old man amid a group of students and filed out into the colonnade. He returned to the notice boards to take down the details of the Ashbery reading so that he could casually mention it to Elizabeth.

"Hey!" said a bright voice behind him. He turned to see her smiling at him again over the folders and books she clutched to her chest, her hair and earrings still luminous in the morning light. Those pentagram earrings which had caused him to believe she must like the same bands that he scrawled on his rucksack and notepads, and had resulted in his disastrous first attempt at engaging conversation. "Are you walking to American Lit.?" She asked again, with that same inviting twist of the shoulders.

"What?" he uttered, frowning involuntarily at her.

"Late night, was it?" she laughed, setting the earrings jiggling again.

"Sorry, I, erm…" he floundered. What the hell was going on?

"You look a bit spaced out," said Elizabeth. "One too many in the Union Bar, was it? I just wondered if you wanted to walk with me to the seminar. You are coming, aren't you?"

"Erm, I think so," said Henry, looking about him. The old professor stepped through the large wooden doors and stopped smartly. He raised his arm in a brisk, military fashion, glanced at his wristwatch, smiled at Henry, and set off purposefully down the steps.

"Listen," said Henry, as he and Beth set off together across the quad, "John Ashbery is giving a reading in a couple of weeks; do you fancy it?"

Dragon Story Time

Brenda Shrewsbury

"Once upon a time," she began.

"Why, Gannie?" Four year old Jacob asked.

"Why what?" she sighed.

"Pon time Gannie, why pon time?" She could almost hear the cogs turning in his very active little brain after he had asked the why question yet again. "Well Jacob it's how stories begin. A story has to have a beginning." She held her breath waiting for the next why. It didn't come; instead he put his much loved, well sucked thumb into his mouth and snuggled closer into her side. The pair of them were rammed tight into their favourite armchair. He was dressed in yet another superhero costume. Captain America this time and as she gazed down at his bright copper curls she thought perhaps her heart really would break if anything were to happen to this precious, precious boy. Removing said thumb from mouth Jacob commanded "More story, Gannie." So with a catch in her breath and only a hint of a wobble in her voice she returned to her story.

"Once upon a time in a land far, far away there lived an old and protective granny dragon who had a handsome and brave young grandson". "Like me and you, Gannie" he interrupted, contorting himself in the small space to gaze up at her. She looked down into his, oh so clear blue eyes and wondered if she could perhaps just get lost in that look, if only time could stand still and they could stay locked like that forever. "You're old Gannie!" Jacob asserted. "Well that's true Jacob but not as old as the granny dragon, she was as old as time itself. Shall I get on with the story?" He nodded his consent, returned thumb to mouth and so she continued.

"The granny dragon and the little boy dragon had many adventures. They lived by the sea and every day they would go to the beach to catch fish for their tea. Well, the granny caught the fish while the grandson played on the beach. Do you know what his favourite game was, Jacob?" She paused while there was a solemn nodding of the head, removal of the thumb and the breathless announcement "Dumpers and diggers in the sand". She smiled. "Well there were no dumpers and diggers in those far off times, but the boy dragon could

110

build the most wonderful sandcastle. He would collect, seaweed, shells, and all manner of flotsam and jetsam and with very little help, as if by magic a whole village of sand buildings would appear."

"Did the daddy dragon help when he came back?" asked Jacob. "My daddy is the bestest maker and my mummy can sing good. She sing me Puff the Magic Dragon at bedtime. It's our most special song!" There was a pause after this solemn pronouncement while she gathered her thoughts. A small elbow in her ribs prompted her to start again.

"Well if you remember Jacob the mummy dragon and the daddy dragon had for some very mysterious reason had to leave the land where the Granny and the little boy dragon lived. They had made the granny dragon take a sacred oath to always love and protect their son, who they just knew was going to grow up into a wonderful, kind, brave and handsome dragon. And in the fullness of time when he was all grown up he would look after his granny."

"Would he catch the fish when he was growd up?"

"Indeed he would Jacob and the granny would sit in her rocking chair on the beach and watch him!"

"No, no, no Gannie, that's silly!" She smiled as she asked "Why?"

"Dragons' are too big to sit in rocking chairs!" came the response.

"Well, you've forgotten the magic that the boy dragon could do. He would, when the time came, be able to make the biggest, most comfy of rocking chairs for his granny. I bet he would even be able to fit in it with her".

Round eyed he looked up at her and asked tearfully "and the mummy and daddy dragon too, Gannie?" She swallowed hard. "No Jacob, remember the mummy and daddy dragon had gone far away to another magical land." His tears came then, he struggled from her side onto her lap and burying his head into her chest he sobbed "Like my mummy and my daddy." Gathering him to her and rocking in her own pain as well as his she began to sing "Puff the Magic Dragon Lived by the Sea".

111

Pride

Pride

Jane Barron

Thrashed and beat he returned,
Feet dragging, body bent
But despite the pain
He had learned
That principals mattered.
And that had lent strength
To his budding muscles
Added length to his skinny arms
Reaching to strike like a hammer,
Their noses and chins and his own
aching, breaking, torn and bruised.
But he didn't lose. He had earned
Respect in defeat -
Wouldn't give in.
They walked away in the end
They wouldn't spend time
Saying he was too easy and small to smash
When he got home
Pride uncurled his back.

Cherry and Glory Pride

Lois Elsden

I love my sister Cherry, she's three minutes younger than me so I'm the eldest. I love her but I have to say I feel eclipsed by her, sort of put in the shade...put in the shade is actually a good way of expressing it since she's blond and sunny and I'm dark and gloomy... well actually I'm not gloomy, I just have the sort of face where people are forever saying 'cheer up' when I'm actually quite happy but just thinking about things.

This is an example: we got our reports and our parents' friends were staying and they were saying to their friends how brilliantly Cherry had done. So the mum said, and how did Glory do, and mum said oh she always does well... as if always doing well was not as good as doing brilliantly...what she meant was I always get a better report than Cherry...well I get a better report in exam results, not necessarily in the other stuff.

Cherry is so nice and lovely to everyone, and she's really popular, everyone likes her - and she doesn't even try to be popular like some people do, she's just liked by everyone. The only person who doesn't like her, although she pretends she does, is Glynis who has her own little group of friends, a clique I guess you'd call it, and has a rich family so she has hangers-on because things like her birthday parties are always much more lavish than the ordinary sort of parties us ordinary sort of children have.

And people say 'Cherry, what a lovely name... is it spelt Cherie? Is it short for Cheryl?' even though both Cherie and Cheryl are exactly the same number of letters...and no, her name is Cherry. With me they say 'oh Glory, I guess that's short for Gloria?' Well, no actually, my name is Glory...it's all due to a mistake either by my dad or the registrar because I was going to be called Gloria, but thankfully there was some sort of muddle and my actual birth certificate, and my baptismal certificate both say Glory - I think the vicar quite liked it.

Cherry is always good, I don't mean in a goody-two-shoes sort of way, but she just always is - I don't mean I'm not good, I don't try to be naughty or do the wrong thing, but sometimes I'm thinking of something and I sort of forget the other thing I'm supposed to do, or sometimes I'm reading a book and then mum says why haven't you made your bed, or you're supposed to be doing your homework, or why did you leave your boots all muddy...as if I had deliberately thought 'oh, I know, I'll leave my bed all in a muddle' or ' actually won't do my homework, now' or 'what a good idea to leave my boots all covered with mud right where mum is going to trip over them...'

Dad gave me a talking to...if your sister can remember to do things, why can't you...she tries to be helpful to mum and after all mum does for you don't you think you're old enough now to be taking responsibility for yourself? It's not Cherry's fault that she remembers stuff and does it when she's supposed to, that's just the way she is... And like last exam time, Dad got quite cross because I wasn't revising, but what was the point when I knew it already. He said I couldn't possibly...except I did and got really good results. Now this seems as if I'm blaming Cherry but honestly I got a bit fed up when Dad said well done to her, and to be honest she'd flunked her maths (but you really tried hard, Cherry, said Dad) and she'd not done as well as me, and Dad said to me, you got away with it this time, Glory - make sure you do your revision properly next exams...

You see what I mean...

Two Haiku on the Theme of Pride

Sue Johnson

In shimmering heat
Feline power lies sleeping
Flies feast on remains

Amaryllis stands
Resplendent in scarlet coat
Face set against wind

Northern Roots

Elizabeth Lawrence

"Look! The lights of Middlesbrough!" My dad would exclaim, as we were nearing the end of our long journey from Cornwall, having set off before dawn and often travelling for twelve hours or more. As with pilgrims of old, the multitude of lights were our only sign of life and a beacon on dark roads. I imagined settlements and tribes, and our tribe eagerly awaiting our arrival. These journeys were long and arduous with a sense of having traversed the length of the country, with its changing landscape, climate and dialects, with much information and history from our parents en route. I was always fascinated by the names of towns such as Cirencester, Leicester, Grimsby and Barnsley with their straight and long, connecting Roman roads; church spires, villages, Nottingham forest and tales of Robin Hood. Pre-motorways, there was always much discussion of routes and ring roads, and my grandad once famously said, "you'll never get through York!" This became a family saying as we imagined an iron curtain and border controls. The first land mark of home was the familiar, dramatic outline of the Cleveland Hills as my mother sang, "Black Hills of Dakota". And the lights of Middlesbrough, twinkling a welcome home.

I was born in the North Riding of Yorkshire, and my northern pride comes from a strong identity and a past rooted in traditions. The Frozen North, as we called our north eastern part of the world, conjured up magical images of The Snow Queen, to children. Snow storms came as early as October and could last until April. Snowflakes descended, as large as saucers, with spiralling patterns against a black night sky. And snow quickly banked outside front doors, blocking paths and driveways. Being snowed-in was a regular occurrence and thick ice and icicles could last the entire winter.

I remember shivering violently in those days, as my mother coaxed me to dress on cold mornings, doing her best to warm our clothes on the hearth; a hard icy frost made swirling patterns on the insides of windows. There were fireplaces in most rooms, and chimney sweeps made a good living, as well as being great entertainment for spectating children. Glowing cheeks, red noses, great overcoats and a well-stocked winter woollen's drawer, stuffed full with hats, scarves and gloves, were the mark of each winter; along with roaring fires, steaming kitchens and every attempt at keeping houses and bodies warm.

The extreme cold and deep snow was part of our northern identity, "you have to be tough to live up north" we would say, and there was an element of truth in that, a tenacity and resilience, but also warm-hearted hospitality, unequal to anywhere else in my experience.

Steeped in northern working class traditions, the men were hard-working and beer-drinking – but they were family-minded, and did their duty by their wives and children, bringing home a weekly wage, usually from the steel works, the main employers at that time. Stereotypical roles, yes, but there was respect for women, and my family was matriarchal. My grandmother ran a tight ship where everyone was looked after; there was pride in the home and enjoyment of life. Employment was high in the town and so was morale.

I shut my eyes and can still hear northern chatter, in the slightly singsong Geordie lilt – it speaks to me of home, love and comfort; and my grandmother bustling in the kitchen with her ever-running commentary. The flat vowels still sound more natural to me, and seem part of the repartee and simple directness of the people, as opposed to the elongated southern vowels – 'pretentious' say inverted snobs, which I disagree with; after all, we each have our own roots; and I adapted, after a while, to fit in down south. Witty and humorous, with a joie de vivre, my relatives laughed a lot and had ready smiles – a gregarious people; often not understanding the shyness and reserve of southerners - 'southern softies'!

Only a hundred and fifty miles from Scotland, many Scottish words and sayings had crept into the northeast dialect. Children were bairns, and often bonnie or canny (with the cute meaning). "Och" was frequently used to exclaim disagreement, and aye for yes – 'why aye!' Boys and girls were lads and lasses; and wives affectionately referred to as 'our lass'. Tightly screwed newspaper used to light fires, were 'faggies'.

The local football team was a source of great pride and most men would go to the match on a Saturday; fathers and sons, down the generations. Violence and hooliganism were unknown and families watched the game in safety. And for the following week the conversation would be dominated by the results of the match, and cause for celebration or commiseration in the pubs.

As part of the steel works, Middlesbrough boasted a transporter bridge across the River Tees, there being only two in the country at that time. We children were thrilled to join the lorry queues in our family car and journey across the murky river. Pride comes in many forms!

There was understandable pride in the magnificent and majestic Cleveland Hills; with Roseberry Topping its one official mountain; it took much endurance to reach the summit, but the panoramic views stretching over hundreds of miles made it worthwhile. Always wonderful to escape to the hills and lie back on a mattress of purple heather to experience the utter peace of a still summer's day, broken only by the occasional bleat from sheep and the lazy drone of bees. The tranquillity has been unmatched anywhere else, since. James Herriot country, the famous Yorkshire vet and author; and the dales are as beautiful as he portrayed in his wonderful autobiographies. Undulating hills, farms, streams, waterfalls and stepping-stones add charm to little tucked-away villages and hamlets. Thick snow in winter brings striking beauty but also isolation as the roads become impassable. The range of hills are landmarks and each hill has its own name – the most famous probably being Captain Cook's with a monument to celebrate the local hero. We drove for miles as a family along winding roads with frequent stops to open and shut gates, denoting farmers' land and keeping sheep enclosed.

The nearest seaside towns are Scarborough, Whitby, Marske, Redcar and Saltburn, stretching miles along a usually very windy and golden coastline. The anticipation of setting off to the seaside with bucket and spade, and the eventual, enticing glimpse of a dark and rough northern sea, topped with white surf was a whole new and exciting world. I never managed more than a paddle before near hypothermia set in; but the bracing air and liveliness of a traditional seaside town with donkey rides, promenades, deckchairs and sand in sandwiches made a wonderful day out, with grandparents, aunts and uncles making up the numbers.

Despite heavy industry and often an acrid smell in the air from the steel works, we had easy access to nature and cleaner air. A constant source of natural beauty was Stewart Park, with magnificent, mature trees, a lake, a café, and a museum featuring Captain Cook's voyage to Australia; Captain Cook was a local hero and a boyhood inspiration to my dad, who eventually emigrated to Australia. When it snowed the park became a winter wonderland of

Narnia-like trees and brilliant whiteness for miles – like walking through a snow forest.

Respectability was very important to my grandparents' generation, marrying in the 1930s during the Depression and then the Second World War, life was a struggle in many ways. And to raise oneself up out of impoverished backgrounds became a driving force.

My grandparents were proud to live in a council house, only allocated to working tenants. They were solidly built from red brick, with well-kept gardens, greens and flower borders tended by the council. Net curtains were a gleaming white and regularly starched; the front step washed and polished to the same cheerful brick red as the houses. I have memories of running up the path into the arms of grandparents, with a "hello lovely, don't slip on the step!" – always too late, from my grandfather, and a "hello beauty" from my grandmother, bustling in the 'back kitchen', with kettle on the hob and clatter of best china as the table was set for tea. My sister and I felt like little princesses with a royal welcome. A roaring fire of 'blazers' my grandfather would proudly announce, as he held newspaper in front to suck up enormous flames that danced and warmed the room. And of course, 'best butter' had to be softened next to the fire before spreading on white bread. The bedrooms were usually cold but with piled up eiderdowns and a couple of hot water bottles warming our nightclothes, and after cocoa and biscuits, we stayed warm all night.

There was great pride in always being neat and tidy; shoes polished, coats brushed with a clothes brush always on a shelf by the hallway mirror. Brylcreemed hair, Old Spice aftershave, a trilby hat and a neat overcoat completed my grandfather's attire.

My grandmother and aunts mostly wore neat, knee-length skirts or dresses, blouses, cardigans, nylon stockings and smart court shoes with a two or three inch heel. Handbags, scarves and gloves completed the outfit, with a dab of perfume behind the ear – usually lavender, eau-de-cologne or Tweed. And then an application of powder and lipstick, always kept in smart handbags with a comb, mirror and lace handkerchief.

Clothes were mended promptly and there was shame in a missing button or a hem hanging. Darning socks was an ongoing task, and shoes were polished until they shone. Men and women wore hats; men doffing them in deference or greeting, and removing them indoors; but women mostly wore hats all the time, setting off their outfits most fetchingly.

At the end of his working life, my grandfather was a clerk in a firm of solicitors, and always a dutiful and conscientious worker. He was the first white collar worker in his family, intelligent and with many hidden talents. He was very musical and played light classical music by ear on the piano. My grandmother also had an innate appreciation of classical music, particularly Chopin. Ironing was always accomplished to the sound of music from the sturdy gramophone, usually on a Friday, listening to 'Friday night is music night!" The upright piano in the front room was their pride and joy – well polished and frequently played. The piano stool was the first piece of elegant furniture I had come across, with its ornate handles and heavy lid, holding old music sheets and songs from a bygone age. The stool was strictly reserved for sitting at the piano.

My grandfather could also draw and paint, in delicate water colours. Despite a shy and retiring nature, he wrote and performed in comedy and musical plays for the RAFA club where he was the welfare officer, deriving great satisfaction from helping people, especially the disabled or widowed.

My grandmother also worked full time in the department store Binns, a House of Fraser. She always wore a black jumper and skirt, with a pearl necklace. Working, for my grandmother, was necessary to the family income, but also meant occasional treats, and a sense of purpose and mixing with the world. She particularly enjoyed working with young people and would tell amusing stories about the latest junior's escapades.

My grandmother had two days off per week; the first day was spent cleaning the house from top to bottom and doing the laundry; and the second, baking for the following week. The vacuuming and dusting was a job my grandfather took pride in each Sunday and we had to follow exact instructions if we were allowed to help.

My grandmother, small and dainty - about four feet and nine inches tall, washed all the bedding and clothes in the wash-house, situated

in the back yard. Standing on a stool she filled a large sink with soap powder and boiling water from a gas boiler, tossing and agitating the clothes before rinsing and wringing them with her small hands, she then fed them through a mangle. Outside drying days were marvellous in the strong northern winds with a long washing line and a tall, wooden clothes prop, raising the clothes as high as roof tops. Otherwise, wooden clothes horses were put to use in the warm kitchen.

The baking was a joy and delight to behold! Aromatic custard tarts with vanilla and nutmeg, coffee and walnut cake, rich chocolate cake and icing laced with rum for extra shine and flavour; Bakewell tarts, fruit pies – the favourite being bilberry pie with fruit gathered from the moors. Blue lips and tongues were part of the season!

My strongest food memories are centred around Christmas, with hospitality, generosity and merrymaking knowing no bounds! I still remember the smell of the cold pantry, storing cooked meat, bread, cakes and cheese. Flagons of the coldest, tangiest lemonade with a sharp fizz and a stone stopper, were kept on the floor, alongside milk. Christmas cake was topped with marzipan only, in the northern tradition, and Christmas puddings studded with sixpences. A very spicy homemade ginger wine was always part of the season, along with piccalilli, dates, figs, nuts and jellied fruit. And everyone, anywhere, wished everyone a Merry Christmas! Merry was the intent.

One year with snow falling, a little girl was delivered to us late on Christmas Eve. My sister and I had almost given up hope of her arrival, looking out constantly onto a dark and empty street, before finally seeing her walking through the snow with her father, clutching his hand and so small against his large frame and overcoat. He was my father's colleague and with his wife in hospital there were too many children to care for; so I had a ready-made sister for a while and loved her fiercely, becoming a surrogate mother at age six. She started infant school while living with us and I tried to protect her at all times. She returned home after a while and we lost touch with the whole family.

New Year's Eve was the main celebration, with singing in the pubs starting early and spilling onto the streets. As children we would be snuggled up in bed listening to the revellers with occasional glimpses out of the window. Just before midnight there was a hush and outside most houses could be seen a man, as tall, dark and handsome as the family could provide, clutching a lump of coal, 'first footing' at midnight. And for the next few days, we would hear men being sent out to let in the New Year for single occupants. Each year, my great aunt, war-widowed as a young bride, would await the arrival of my grandad, her brother in law, and wouldn't go out until he had been.

Entertainment abounded all year round. People regularly threw parties at home with buffets, music and dancing; and often very merry but never drunk, in my recollection. Dances with big bands, bingo halls, working men's clubs and cinemas were plentiful in the lively town.

Whatever changes have taken place in the Middlesbrough that was, it will always be part of my memories and early childhood roots; and all the characters in my family stay with me in thought as a source of strength and inspiration.

The Seventh Deadly Sin; or is it?

Brenda Shrewsbury

What, she wondered, would it take for them to say it? Today of all days would be a great place to start. Ideal in fact. Was it because they considered it a sin? Perhaps, she pondered, it was because it was an emotional response and God knows, they did not do emotions.

Growing up she had considered that they were a "nice, normal family." She smiled to herself as she realised in her head she had placed inverted commas around that statement. It had been as she began her torturous journey through her adolescence (a journey that was ridiculously late compared to her peers), that she realised they were far from the norm.

She was sixteen before she began to feel the rebellion of thoughts and deeds that her contemporaries had been talking about, stropping and acting out, for at least four of the proceeding years. Where had that revolt got her? Her insurgence, mild as it was, had caused them such anguish and pain she soon abandoned her flirtation with sex, drugs and rock and roll!

She mentally snorted at the memory of her attempts to blend in, to be like everybody else. She could still feel the burning shame of not knowing what to do in the back yard of the grottiest pub in town. She had been led there willingly enough by a spotty youth, name long forgotten. The mortification as he pressed her up against the wall, forced his tongue into her mouth and his knee into her groin. Perhaps on reflection biting his tongue had not been the kindest of responses but it had been very effective!

Then there was her, as they referred to it at the time, "abhorrent taste for illegal substances". She recalled that her said flirtation with alcohol had by most adolescent experimentation been extremely brief. She really had not liked the vomiting in the street that the consumption of a pint of snake bite and a half of Guinness had induced and as for Gin, Whiskey and Vodka, the taste had been totally vile. Where then, she pondered, had she acquired her now firmly entrenched love of fine wines? As for the "evils of smoking," well, both tobacco and weed had produced such paroxysms of eye watering coughing that, to quote the youth of today, why would she voluntarily "go there!" She had soon, of her own free will, given them up as a bad idea, even though her so-called friends of the time derided her with taunts of "Chicken"! How many of them were now fighting cigarette addiction or, worse still, lung cancer? As for hard drugs, the thought of the induced loss of control had terrified her and as she was positively phobic about needles the whole shebang was a no-no!

Rock and Roll, now that had been her "thing". She could lose herself in the music, identify with the words, and be moved to joy or despair by the sounds of so many of the musicians and bands of her day and earlier. Her parents' complete bewilderment of this "so called music" was the wedge that she wilfully chose to drive into the family unit. She fought against her father's long and torturous explanation as to why she should not find "that noise" enjoyable, meaningful or worth her time, energy and obvious musicality. Oh how little they had understood her; or, she realised now, how little she had understood herself. Her mother had the clincher though. "How could she abuse her God-given talent by playing and enjoying the devil's music, especially when she knew what pleasure they as a family derived from the classical and ecclesiastical music they played together and had dedicated their life and spirituality to?"

In the end, she had been unable to endure their pain and anguish and her teenage rebellion was over before it had really begun. She did their bidding, she knuckled down, returned to church, and studied and practised and then studied and practised some more. Oh, the endless hours of practice. Where, at the end of the day, had that really gotten her? Even playing with The London Philharmonic had only garnered a gruff "well done". So she wrote her rock songs, she blended the sounds of her classical training with the rock rhythms of her heart and the words and melodies had flowed from her mind to the page with an ease that astounded her.

The deal she struck with a recording company had been the brain child of her dearest and truest friend, and the mystique of this incredible talent that would not perform live, or give interviews, who insisted on complete anonymity, had been born.

For years she did not have the courage to disappoint them, tell them that she was living their dream not hers. Now though as she stood in the wings at one of, if not the most prestigious of concert venues in

127

the world, her heart, without any help from them, swelled with pride. Yes some of it was for herself, she could not, would not deny, but mostly it was pride for her music, her band, consisting of some of the finest musicians she knew, her son, her daughter and her dear, dear, trusted husband.

The evening's compere asked the audience to make some noise, to welcome the incredible talent that was Mystic Pride to the stage. She stole a glance at her parents, both standing to the side of her, ramrod straight with identical looks of complete bewilderment on their faces. One last chance she thought; nothing, just two tight smiles. Your loss, she thought, as she walked, head held high, onto the Pyramid stage.

Wood

Stone Love

Sue Johnson

She wore the darkness as a cloak
enfolding her in a velvet embrace.

A warm breeze unfurled sensuous
green fingers towards her bare shoulders.
Cold feet caressed by sphagnum slippers,
Spotted lichen stockings fastening ochre hues to blemished thighs.

Eyes in the rustling canopy surveyed her form
with an ancient familiarity that she silently accepted,
beckoning her admirer with outstretched hand.

Tendrils of ivy adorned her medusa hair,
slithering over swollen breasts and belly
as she strained to look upon her observer in his ebony lair.

Too late, his feathered form breaks cover,
Gliding away from her solid gaze,
Hooting his derision to the silver moon.

Renewal

Elizabeth Lawrence

Crimson and gold's array
Auburn's tumbling sway
Chestnut brown warm and deep
Smiling pools of laughter
Echoes from my soul

Sheltered beneath branches
Hidden, leaf-veiled from searching rays
Rooted tangled and gnarled
Iron tremors grip the earth
Cleave and snap
In certain finality

Towering to heaven
Whispering into eternity
Roaring an answer to the wind
Majestic power

A language long forgotten
Stirring a response
Hunger made strong
As a new-born's first breath
Renewing from the wood
Growing from the wood

Wood-smoke and blankets
Orange embers glow
Passions flame

Peace of the wood
The wood omnipotent

Decay, rebirth and splendour

The Nutcracker

Macaque

The thatch of thin twigs and bound grasses sieved the noon sun, causing random specks of light to glint in the shadows, tricking the red mud walls out of their feigned grey. The lattice screen over the single doorway was propped open affording a partial view of the village, but there was little to be seen of people or livestock at this time of day.

Inside the hut, the man worked carefully, turning the fragment in his fingers. Like a blind man relying on his sense of touch to recognise a familiar face, he studied the dark object against his pale palms, learning it, communing with it, guessing the form hidden within. Each piece of ebony and sandalwood in the woven basket beside him contained a hidden form, like the kernel of a nut, or a bone caked in mud after the rains. His task was to crack the nut, thumb away the mud, uncover the likeness within the wood.

As he rubbed his thumb along this particular piece, he thought of Obasu, one of the young women of the village. She would pass his hut whenever she ventured to the neighbouring town, and he thought of her now, balancing, as she often did, a bundle of clothes or a water jar on her head, the accomplished act accentuating her statuesque profile against the bright, low horizon. Obasu's profile, complete with clothing bundle soon took shape in his hands as he uncovered her from her timeless vault within the heart of the wood, his short chisel delicately excavating and refining her. When he knew that she was finished, fully uncovered, he set her down on the square board in front of him, where she took her place among the rest of the tribe. He had already carved two huts, like his own but slimmer by proportion, the conical roof more elongated. This theme of elongation continued with two giraffes, the long mask of a witch doctor, and now Obasu with her towering bundle. Among these figures were distributed eight sandalwood lions and seven ebony monkeys. He took a sip of water from his tin mug, then picked up the basket to search for another monkey.

In the shop on the busy street, the traffic was muffled by the thick glass, the fan heater over the door, and the heavy scent of the different woods. Something rhythmic was quietly audible, seeming to emanate from the furniture and statuary surrounding the boy. His father was interested in a carved wooden chess set displayed on a low, solid table near the window. The board looked thick and heavy, intricately detailed with vines and leaves around the edge. The chequered effect was produced by an alternation of carved and plain squares, and each of the carved squares depicted an elephant or a lion or a monkey or some less familiar animal, partially hidden by tall grasses. The way the shop light caught the grain of the smooth squares made the carved wood look much darker, so that it hardly registered with the boy that the squares were not in fact black and white.

The playing pieces fascinated the boy, whose father had taught him the rudiments with a standard child's set. Instead of crenelated towers, four thatched huts stood at the corners of the board; instead of horse heads, the long, slender necks of giraffes stood beside men with huge, flat faces. The queen was represented by a curvaceous woman with an enormous headpiece, and the king by a bust with a stark, proud visage. In front of them all, instead of a line of bowling pins, were fierce lions and crouching monkeys, each with a slightly different expression.

While his father examined the pieces, turning them in his fingers, appraising the smooth curves of the queen, the abrasive detail of the thatch, the boy wandered around the rest of the shop, driven by the rhythm of the drums. On one wall, beside a stand of spears, was a large painting of a tribal village. Sparse, twisted trees stood out against the flat, low horizon. In the foreground, a woman with her long skirt gathered in her left hand was balancing a large bundle of clothes on her head, while a slender boy with a long spear walked beside her. In the middle of the picture was a round, thatched hut with a conical roof, and an open door made of dark twigs. The large African sun dominated the pale blue sky, and the hut and foreground seemed to burn red and gold. The boy felt warm just looking at the picture; the colours seemed to shimmer; he could hear the tribal drums, smell the dust and the trees and the thatch. He felt drawn to the open doorway, certain that someone was inside, as if the painter had painted someone he knew well onto the centre of the canvas, and then painted the hut around them, painted the shadows over them, all the while secure in the knowledge that they were there, an unseen yet integral part of the picture. The boy closed his eyes, feeling the heat from the sun on his eyelids, feeling the wind from the plains on his face. He began to visualise a man sitting in the cool shade of the hut, working, turning something small over and over in his hands, feeling the contours with his thumb, smiling.

His father was behind him now, talking to someone. The boy turned as he heard the rich timbre of the stranger's voice.

"I'm sorry, sir, but the picture is not for sale."

Haunting

Webs We Weave

Jane Barron

Jonus was hiding behind the bushes growing untidily beneath a notice board. It advised skippers of the narrow boats on this section of the canal about distances to the locks and so forth. He was agitated and sweating, he knew what he was about to do, and that he was not able to stop himself, but that same lack of control was making him wildly angry, jittery and impatient. He hunkered down and waited for the woman he had seen standing against the skyline before descending to the canal bank towards his hiding place.

It was happening again, this urge that racked his body and nerves with a desire to dominate and experience total sexual release, way beyond any normal or controllable emotions. It had happened only twice before in his life and had had devastating consequences both times – but not for him. He had escaped and cowered in the dark places until he could run far, far away from discovery and responsibility. A woman had died when she could not defend herself from the seemingly polite and intelligent stranger who had turned into a brutal and mindless animal.

That young woman had been entranced by the good looking guy that had she met in the cafe close to her flat, having fancied a latte on her way home. The other girls were waiting there for her, they were going to the gym together after work, and it hadn't seemed a big deal to let him walk with her; he said he was going that way anyway, he must be gallant and see her home.

Unsuspecting, she had strolled with him past the entrance to the walled-off area behind the flats, where the dustbins were kept. Only, what seemed like moments later, filled with tearing and punching and terror, her body damaged and invaded, she had found herself lying on her back among the stinking, rotting food from the overturned waste bins, staring up at the night sky, unable to cry out or move as she felt the life drain from her.

Pat had gone to boot camp last Friday night after work, because despite feeling shattered, she was determined to get fitter and get those couple of pounds off. More irritatingly, her boyfriend Mark had whispered slyly to her in the office,that she couldn't afford to miss the session or she would never have the stamina for the peaks walk.

There were five of them going: Mark, his two walking buddies, whom she knew only vaguely, and the lovely Veronica had asked to join them too, just for a laugh, she had said! This young woman, only lately moved into their branch of the company, with short blond hair and a slim athletic body, announced that yes, she worked out, swam, and played tennis, and just loved walking.

"She said she was an Amazon with never ending stamina, and when she said it, she looked pointedly at him, Jenny, ignoring the fact that I was standing right there! I really hate her! And if I don't go on this Three Peaks challenge, who knows what might happen; men are so gullible."

"Is he really worth it, Pat? He keeps you constantly under pressure to change yourself. You always do stuff that he likes...when did he last ask you what you want to do for the weekend?" Jenny didn't like the way Mark had turned her friend from a funny and relaxed woman into the driven individual who now sat before her. She didn't like the smarmy way Mark had pecked her on the cheek when they met, either.

They had spent the Saturday shopping for the walking trousers and boots Pat would need for the challenge. Pat had kept the boots on to start wearing them in but in fact, they were so comfortable, and her own high boots had been killing her feet anyway, so it was a relief. Then on the way home, Jenny suggested they stop at the wine bar for a quick glass of wine before heading home. They were both ready for it, after the crowded bus ride back from town.

They had had a good laugh and Pat felt relaxed, back to her old self, joking and regaling her friend with the office politics. Jenny was a nursery nurse and a gentle, caring character, she couldn't believe some of the cut and thrust and the ludicrous goings on in Pat's office. They both sipped their wine and recovered from the laughter, when Jenny unexpectedly leaned in close, and with her blue eyes looking deeply into Pat's brown ones, told her friend that it was about time she gave some serious thought to her relationship with Mark, and where was this job going anyway? It was changing her, this was the real Pat, the one she loved, but it was rare to see her much these days.

Pat was surprised by this sudden frankness, but they were close, so she knew Jenny must really be bothered by it.

It was however, time to go and they hugged on the top of the bridge. Jenny waved and continued down the main road while Pat watched her friend for a moment, pondering on that last comment, then, turning right, she started the descent onto the canal bank that ran under the main road and the next. Pat and Mark lived in a flat close to the top of the steps that came up from the canal at the next bridge. It was a short and pleasing cut through from where the bus dropped her each day from the office. The council were clearing all along the canal and the water was reasonably clear, but although all the debris had now been cleared away, the next steps of landscaping the slope up into the canopy of trees and repairing the edges of the canal bank were yet to come. This part of the canal was to be included into the network of usable waterways and she was looking forward to seeing narrow-boats tying up here and tourists improving the local economy of bars and restaurants around the bridges. God knows, the area needed a bit of TLC and life injected into it.

The assault was sudden and violent. He had been crouched, waiting behind the bushes, rushing out at her at the last moment, from the direction of the bridge steps she was aiming for. He grasped her shoulders and his momentum took them both down to the ground, but with lightning speed Pat had brought up her knee and he fell heavily onto it, her reaction stunningly athletic and vigorous, surprising herself as well as her attacker. Even as he bent double, his damaged genitals screaming in pain, he continued the attack, his rage adding impetus to his violence and he clutched onto her arm and a handful of hair, as he rolled sideways, howling in fury.

She rolled with him and, above him now, she was able to get onto her knees astride him. Alive with terror she grabbed on to his filthy clothes as they grappled for domination. He punched her hard, with a sweeping blow to her cheekbone, bringing a shriek of agony as her head shook and pain crashed into her brain. He tore at her clothes as he pushed himself up, taking her with him and throwing her onto her back again.

But he had misjudged her. Pat was a fit and strong young woman, almost as tall as him, and her fear turned to searing anger as her face was pressed and held into his clothes, so rank she wanted to vomit. His hand was down between her legs, tugging at her trousers as he pinned her down with his torso, his breath rancid and revolting.

Fear and loathing lent strength to her limbs and pushing, thrusting with knees, elbows and her body convulsing under him, she managed to crack her forehead onto his lip. The pain took him by surprise and in that moment they became opponents not rapist and victim. The sheer brutish, physicality of the fight that followed between them became, for both, a fight for survival.

They wrestled near the edge of the path, grunting and panting with exertion, until suddenly he lost his balance and she, capitalising on his backward momentum, hurled him from her and into the canal! Falling to her knees, sucking in air, tears running down her cheeks and the breath knocked out of her, she watched him come up, gasping for air, a couple of metres out. Stumbling to her feet in a panic to get away, she slipped and fell heavily onto the canal bank and in a moment he was there grabbing at her ankle.... yanking at her ankle.

Gripped by a frenzy of fear now, Pat was pulled around, her bottom sliding towards the edge of the bank as he tried to pull her in, but bringing back the leg that was still free of his grasp, she kicked out with such force that she felt his nose crack against the solid sole of her walking boot. He went completely berserk as he spat and choked on the blood and water but, terrifyingly, he held onto her ankle. She kicked out again and again and again, sobbing and shouting, even long after his grip had loosened, until she was exhausted and sickened. He slid beneath the water.

Her breathing slowed, the surface of the water remained still.... and it was over, as suddenly as it had begun. She stayed in that position for a while, in shock and barely believing what had gone before, until, beginning to shiver, she realised the consequences of what she had done. It would only be much later that she would recognise and acknowledge to herself why going to the police had been out of the question. For now, she stood, and, glancing quickly around, found and gathered up her shopping and handbag. She hurried towards the steps leading up to the road and their flat only two houses down.

When she opened the door, she was dishevelled, but by now in control of herself, only to find Mark dressed smartly and reeking of aftershave, about to go out. Although disconcerted by her appearance, he was quite obviously a bit irritated to be held up. Pat began to explain what had happened, but as soon as she mentioned the canal path and he glanced down at the wet muddied knees and hands, he had just sneered. He told her in a patronising tone, that if she was stupid enough to use the canal path at night, she deserved to fall over and was lucky not to have gone straight into the filthy water.

She had looked at him incredulously, silenced by his coldness and especially so, as he slipped past her, without another glance, telling her not to wait up, adding nastily, that the others were waiting to discuss the challenge at the pub, and he wasn't going to wait for her to change, when she had allowed herself to be so late. The door closed behind him and again she found herself standing mute and alone wondering what had just happened. After a moment or two, she dropped her bags, took off the walking boots and dropping her clothes on the bedroom floor, stepped into the shower.

Later, she sat on the edge of the bed after her phone call to Jenny. Pat had given her friend a surprisingly brief and inaccurate account of the attack, for as soon as she began to speak, Pat regretted that she had called at all. However, Jenny had calmed her, angrily denouncing the man. "If he came out of the bushes and then fell in the canal, that was his own fault and he probably climbed out again further down the bank anyway. In fact, are you sure he didn't watch you and see which house you went into Pat?"

Pat allowed her friend to understate the reality of it all, even encouraged it, almost believing with her, that the whole thing had been just an unfortunate wrong place, wrong time moment. Putting the phone down, Pat stared at the boots then forced herself to pick them up. They had been lying there all the time and Pat knew there was blood on them. She knew that there would have been no climbing out of the canal.

She curled up on the bed, drawing her knees up to her chest and clasped her arms around them. She had changed into her nightclothes automatically after the shower, but a definite decision had to be made about telling the police...or not. Although still in a kind of shock, her mind was gradually beginning to process the events of the last couple of hours.

She pictured Mark walking out without caring about her at all. She pictured his face if she told him the truth, he would accuse her of extreme retaliation, or wild exaggeration, and she knew without a doubt, that he would somehow blame her for being there in the first place. She imagined his mocking face at work telling everyone that the police would have to dredge the canal whether they believed there might be a body or not.

She tried to imagine how she would explain the state of his face, neck and shoulders, to the police when the body was found. How would she explain the terrifying blood lust she had felt coursing through her brain as she pulped his face with her boots. Explain that after the intense battle with him, there was an actual exhilaration in the act of killing him.....and pure satisfaction of seeing him sink under the water. The loss of control was not fear, at the end it was choice, and it made her very afraid.

And she suddenly saw Mark for exactly who he was! She saw through Jenny's eyes the arrogant and mean character lurking under that assured attitude, and his preoccupation with his own good looks. Sitting up, Pat looked around the bedroom, at the shared life that was not really shared at all. It was late, nothing to be done tonight she thought with complete clarity. She would tell him she was too sore to go to work tomorrow and then she would pack and leave. She had no other ties to the area, she would get on a train taking only her big suitcase, she would leave the rest of her bits and pieces for Mark to keep or get rid of. She would decide where to go tomorrow, get settled, then she would call Jenny. She had savings and a degree, she would get work, her life would start again but taking off at a completely different tangent.

Pat would think about the man later...no one knew the truth, even if a body had turned up, she was not implicated, and anyway, she would be long gone. So she was going to let it lie. She thought the danger was past. Pat could not have known, that she would never be free of him...

The Three Mummers

Lois Elsden

I've been pondering on a mesmerising painting I saw - not in reality but on-line, by the artist David Bez. I'll share links later so you can see some of David's work. I came across David via a particular painting he shared on Twitter - it was so arresting, so engaging, and somehow invaded my thoughts so I haven't been able to stop thinking about it; a story is sure to follow!

The painting which so entranced me is called 'Three Mummers'. It's quite small in real life, 21 x 18 inches and is painted in acrylic and oil on paper; David adds: #Folklore Thursday, customs and rituals (links later). The colours are mostly browns and shades of brown, with some black, and then some cloudy blue skies.

You might guess from the title that there are three mummers, and yes, there are three mysterious figures. Mummers, in case you don't know, are traditional players also known as guisers, who perform almost ritualistic plays dating back to the middle ages (and probably beyond). Ordinary folk dress up and, in bands, go round villages, often from pub to pub, enacting these old stories, usually of a fight involving St George but other figures too; someone is killed but revived by The Doctor...There are scenes involving mummers in Thomas Hardy's Return of The Native, and in Ngaio Marsh's detective story, 'Off With His Head'.

The three figures in David Bez's pictures are difficult to make out... are they actually human? David has painted some other pictures with strange creatures - maybe people, maybe not, in a series called 'Ceremonies in the Wilderness'.

In the foreground, the land is marked with strange symbols - or are they just natural features which look like symbols and runes? The mid-ground has what looks like a bank with maybe brambles, maybe undergrowth, and a large old tree, gnarled and standing like a giant Ent. The figures are standing staring at us, on the track either coming towards us, or about to leave, but looking back before they go. Or maybe they will pass along beside the bank and disappear off to the left following the trail.

The track goes on behind them, between the Ent-like tree and what might be dead winter brambles...or might not. In the distance a pale peak of a mountain rises, catching the light of dawn or the last light of dusk - or is it not a mountain but a cloud? The sky is darkly cloudy but there are blue patches behind, bright blue. The clouds appear to be moving, moving across the picture towards the right.

The figures, the three figures, tall and strange, upright animals, or human, or half-human? They may all be holding staffs, certainly the one in the centre is. The etiolated one on the left seems to have horns - very straight and pointy, and the only creature I can find with such horns is a type of gazelle, a South African gazelle called a gemsbok. The central figure, more stocky and seeming to be wearing a coat, cloak or smock, appears to have three horns - or is it a hat? His staff is short like a walking stick. The figure on the right is standing a little forward of the others, and he seems to be gesturing, or maybe speaking - but of course in a picture you can't hear words, only imagine them. Maybe he doesn't have horns, maybe he has the ears of a hare, in fact his face - what you can make out, almost seems as if it is shaped like the muzzle of a hare.

When I first saw the picture I stared at the screen for quite a while, and I thought, *"So mysterious - are they threatening or do they bring good fortune? Are they leaving or arriving? Standing or dancing?"* Who knows!

Haunting 101

Fenja Hill

"Ok, I know you're all anxious to get out there and get started, but we need to go through this briefing first. It's not as easy as you imagine, and it wouldn't be the first time that a bucket of ectoplasm has been delivered to me to sort out, after a failed attempt by someone who wasn't paying attention at this stage.

"First, I'll address the three basic questions that always come up at this point.

"One. Some of you are not sure why you're here. You are here because, while you were alive, this is what you thought would happen after you died. Generally, you either wanted to go back and be a comforting, caring presence for someone you loved, or you wanted to go back and make life difficult for someone you were angry with. Whichever it was, you wanted it enough to affect the next stage of your existence. Right now, there are others being briefed on reincarnation, various versions of heaven and hell, and a bunch of other options. Whatever they believed while they were alive, that's what's coming next for each of them.

"Two. Why do you need a briefing? Surely haunting is just a matter of walking through walls and making creepy noises? No, it's not that simple. I can't count the number of times I've been called out to rescue someone whose lapse in concentration has left them firmly entrenched half-way through a door or wall, causing havoc to the people living in the building. And you also need to understand that, unless you organised your own deaths and made sure they happened exactly where you wanted them to, you are likely to find that, having decided on haunting, you're stuck haunting a random stranger, because your "ghost identities", for want of a better word, will be tied to the place where you died.

"Yes, yes, I know, it's not what you anticipated. Well, you should have done some research before settling on this for your afterlife choice.

"And three. Can you change your minds now that you know the reality? No, you can't. You wanted to haunt someone, so you will haunt someone. Some of you thought that if you hovered around your wife, husband, partner, friends, and kept yourself in their hearts and minds, they wouldn't move on, find new love, get over you. You'll be disappointed to find that your selfishness was a waste of time, because the files I have here indicate that they were nowhere near you when you died, so you'll be haunting ... let's see ...a zebra crossing in Camden Town, the kitchen department of Bristol Ikea, a shoe shop in Aberdeen, a mattress – oh yes, Colin, I'm afraid your mattress was taken to the dump and burned, so you'll be floating around the municipal tip. Still, we don't all get the things we dreamed of.

"Shelley and Asif, you will both get to haunt your murderers, because your deaths were very hands-on, so you'll be fine. You may eventually, however, become bored with the idea of revenge. What can I say? You were angry, they were killing you, I suppose it wasn't a time to be logical, but it's out of my hands. Or it would be, if I had any.

"Ok, we'll take a short break now, and then Sharon will come in and start you off with some very simple materialising, before going on to moving through solid objects. Also, for those of you who want to make noises, please think about exactly what sounds you will need, because once you've chosen them, you can't change. The clank of chains can become tiresome after a few hundred years, and wailing isn't easy to maintain after the first few days; you'll find it fades to a bit of a mumble unless you put all your psychic energy into it, and if you do that, you're likely to lose focus and get stuck in a wall.

"Good luck everyone. Happy haunting."

The Silent Valley

Elizabeth Lawrence

In the misty mellowness of a late October morning, the smell of wood smoke and coal fires lingering in the valley air, a heavy dew on the grass and leaves, with just enough sun to catch a glimpse of bronzed bracken on the mountain tops, bird song promised yet another golden autumnal day.

The town was waking up to its usual burst of morning activity; children walked, ran or skipped to school, mostly in groups with friends and siblings, and mothers held the hands of infants. The sense of purpose and optimism was palpable, as women hummed their way through washing and cleaning in their contented, busy lives, in a community of high employment with generations of pride, identity and continuity.

The coal slurry was always a looming, ominous threat, shrouding the soft green mountainous beauty and tainting the heather-sweet air. The people were unaware of the dormant danger, and accepted the heavy, black mountain cap as part of their lives and livelihood; trusting in managers' health and safety checks, as their children were schooled under the coal mountain's towering darkness.

The cheerful teachers ordered the usual straight lines and silence as the crocodile of children trustingly entered the inner school. Mothers pegging out washing and scrubbing steps were reassured to hear the familiar sound, rising from the valley, of children singing in high and clear voices, 'All things bright and beautiful'. "At 9.15 a.m. it started as a tremendous rumbling sound; everyone froze". After the slide there was total silence - instant death to some; final, unrelenting, trapped suffocation, numbness and shock to others. The old valley sounds never returned; buried under the slurry, along with the innocence and brightness of the young.

Then the sounds of a community out to frantically save - shovelling, drilling, carrying; women screaming, shouting, being restrained and fainting. Children sobbing, being carried; and so many ashen faces in shock. After the first few bodies were found, the rescuing process became a nightmarish task which took a degree of determination and numbness. Men and women dug and tunnelled, continuing, even when all hope had died; but not knowing where else to take their anguish.

And the children forgot how to play, robbed of their childhood, guilty to have survived and anxious not to meet the faces of bereaved parents. They sometimes escaped the horror into a land of games and make believe; but never for long, and were always haunted by absent friends at each of life's landmarks

The valley has been haunted for over 50 years now, and will continue until the natural life-span of those taken so unnaturally and tragically will have expired; and those left who remember, laid to rest, hopefully, at peace with their children.

In the memorial garden, with row upon row of small graves, headstones are designed like crib arches, with a cross and an angel over each. Fresh flowers always adorn the plots and the silence is eerie. A multitude of children on this scale is usually associated with a playground filled with laughter and squealing; but their parents still hear them as they sit quietly; some for hours, having nowhere else to vanquish the ghosts.

Mothers still look up at kitchen clocks at 9.00 am, hearing the last strains of singing before the nightmare began. And some still see children hopping and playing, on their way to and from school; but it is only momentary wishful thinking.

Some families lost all their children and were haunted by empty rooms, toys and routines. Marriages broke up, unable to cope with the daily grief in a spouse's face, the futility of trying to find solace and constantly failing.

Being haunted can be a comfort until the agony of realisation cuts relentlessly. And it's a life sentence. Over half the survivors suffered from post-traumatic stress disorder. Aberfan is a valley of nightmares and ghosts. But for the post disaster generations, the ghosts are historic, as life continues.

The human spirit is ever renewing and the mountains regained their beauty and birdsong. Many bridges of humanity were built as the community supported one another and used the disaster to form links to help many causes, which became a solace and an outlet for grief. An important turning point in the healing of the valley was the forming of the community choir. Grief could be expressed and shared, and a thing of beauty created as a tribute to the lost children of Aberfan.

Coventry Road

Macaque

Night. Fire. Faces lit by the flames, eyes lit from within. Fear and frenzy in the eyes, hatred on the lips. A bible gripped tightly, so tightly, trapping god firmly in the pages. There is no god here tonight. Villagers crowd together round the raging flames, shouting, praying, their agitation enhanced by the strobing shadows, the cold night air at their backs, the heat of redemption crackling at their hearts. The witch is brought down the lane, bound and struggling, face pale, eyes like an owl, but the villagers don't see her fear, only the wild eyes of her familiar. The crowd cheers. An ugly noise. A boy lunges awkwardly forward, anger and terror and helplessness in his moon face. He is held back, tears burning to salt in the roar of the flames.

"It was the night of October 31st, 1505, All Hallows Eve; the night of witches and demons. Four of them brought me to that place, bound and trembling, the terror enough to bring on one of my fits. My parents didn't stop them. There was no trial, no sanction, no one to turn to for justice or sense. The only law was that of their ignorance. They lashed me to a thick stake, the blacksmith and his boy, big, strong men, superstitious and weak-minded as babies.

"Only Henry was there in my defence, but what good was one half-wit against a whole village? They were rough with him, tormenting him as usual, threatening to tie him behind me on the stake, accusing him of lying with the devil's daughter. Poor Henry; he didn't understand. But he knew more than they did. Less intelligent and closer to nature than all of them, he knew I was sick. He kept telling them, shouting again and again that I wasn't a witch, shouting even as the four hoisted up the stake and threw me into the middle of the raging flames until the crackling, the searing heat and my own screams drowned out his sweet voice forever."

There was silence in the classroom as Claire retook her seat and straightened her exercise book on the desk. Dust motes danced in the light that angled through the high windows onto the scuffed floor. Students shuffled uncomfortably in their chairs, one or two clearing their throats, glancing at Claire, glancing at the teacher.

"That would have gained you a very good grade for a piece of creative writing, Claire," said Mr Stokes with a harshness belied by his quiet voice, "however, this is History class, not English, and I asked for a factual account. You will redo that for Monday morning."

"This *is* factual, sir," Claire objected, "these events took place. This actually happened to Nora Styles not two miles from here."

"If you were quoting from a source, that should have been made clearer. However, if that were the case, I would be most interested to discover how Nora Styles survived the raging flames and managed to commit the experience to paper." The teacher's snide tone elicited sniggers from the rest of the class. Claire's protests were cut short. "If you continue to argue, Miss Pearson, you can redo the assignment in detention, and also write me 500 words on the difference between fact and fantasy. Now, George, let's hear your factual account, please."

Claire left the History block with Jasmine and Dan in tow. "What's his fucking problem?" She asked angrily, screwing up the detention slip and throwing it into the rusting litter bin by the door.

"He was a bit harsh, I admit," said Jasmine, "but you did stray from the topic a bit."

"I did not! That was a historical account. So what if I wrote it in the first person for dramatic effect? God, talk about the oppression of individuality!"

"Why did you write it like that?" asked Dan as they all sat down on a bench at the side of the playground, rummaging in their bags for their sandwiches. "Nobody else interpreted the assignment that way. I mean, it was really good, you know,"

"You were making it up, weren't you?" interrupted Jasmine.

"No I was not! Look, if I tell you something…" Claire took a breath, and looked at her two friends. "Ok, you cannot repeat this to anyone." Dan and Jasmine shrugged their consent, but Claire's dramatic demeanour was starting to sober them. "I'm serious, guys, I don't want anyone to hear this." Dan took the earphone out of his left ear, and they both nodded and sat looking at her with rapt attention, their sandwiches forgotten for the instant. "Last weekend, well, Friday night, it was after we'd been given the assignment topic – I was coming back from Marci's, we'd had some booze cos her parents were out, and I had a seizure."

"Christ!" exclaimed Jasmine in a hushed tone. "Why didn't you say? Have you seen the doctor?"

"Yeah, usual stuff, you know – no drinking, flashing lights or bungee jumping for six months."

Dan leant towards her, genuinely concerned. "You've not had one for ages; was it bad?"

"It was unusual. I had a vision, or some sort of psychic experience or something. I kind of dreamed – for want of a better word – the whole episode that I wrote for the assignment. But it was deeper, stronger than a dream. I knew Nora's whole life up to that point; I knew all the villagers; I knew about her friendship with Henry, it was like I had her memories; I knew she was epileptic although she didn't have a fit during the burning, and that's why they thought she was possessed. I 'dreamed' it all from her perspective, I never saw her like you see yourself in dreams; everything felt real, from the heat of the flames and the noise, and the smell –"

"Jesus! Christ, calm down, it's alright," said Jasmine.

"Yeah, look, it was only a dream," said Dan.

"It wasn't, though. It actually happened. It all really happened. And right here! Do you realise, if I had been alive then, they would have burned me, *alive*, just for having fits!"

"Alright, look," said Dan, trying to remain rational in spite of the hysteria building up in his friend's voice and stare, "have you ever experienced anything like this before? You know, if you had a fit after watching a film, say? I mean, what are your normal fits like?"

"Yeah," said Jasmine, grasping desperately for some flotsam of security, "what makes you so sure it wasn't just a dream?"

Claire put her bag on the floor in front of her and shuffled closer to her friends. "I looked a few things up when we were doing research for the stupid assignment. You know the field at the top of Coventry Road? By that big oak tree? Well, I looked it up. They really did burn suspected witches there, there's documentary evidence in the library. And haven't you ever seen that field when it's been ploughed? All those black patches in the earth? That's charcoal. The earth remembers those crimes. And now, so do I."

"Ok, you're scaring me now, Claire," said Jasmine. "Is this a wind-up for Halloween or something, yeah?"

Claire took no notice of her, but leant further forward, conspiratorially, and the others mimicked her involuntarily. "I'll tell you something else I found out, no word of a lie: why is it called Coventry Road?" She looked from Jasmine to Dan, who stared back at her, nonplussed. "It doesn't lead to Coventry; it doesn't lead anywhere, it's just a country lane, isn't it? You know, Banwell Road leads to Banwell, Yatton Road leads to Yatton,"

"Who cares? I live on Windermere Crescent but it's nowhere near the fucking Lake District," Dan pointed out.

"That's different, Dan, it's a Crescent, not a road. Same with Avenues and Streets, you can name them after anything, but old road names have geographical significance."

"Listen to the town planning expert, Dan!" said Jasmine, still trying to make light of the way the conversation had turned.

"It used to be called The Coven Tree Road. The villagers believed that oak tree was where a coven of witches held their circles."

"Holy shit!" laughed Dan, pushing Jasmine's shoulder. "She's really lost it now."

"It is a creepy lane, though, isn't it?" said Jasmine, quietly. "You can almost sense -"

"What? The naked hags dancing round their broomsticks on a Saturday night?" laughed Dan, waving his arms about in a parody of ravers.

"I told you this was serious, Dan!" Exclaimed Claire, punching him, but they all laughed, and the tension was broken. The bell sounded for the end of break, and they each put their uneaten sandwiches back in their bags, and moved towards the Science building.

"Hey, will you still come to Simon's party? You know, after detention?" Dan asked as they mingled with the other clusters of students exiting the playground.

"I'm not going to the fucking detention," Claire said contemptuously over her shoulder. "What's Stokes going to do? Burn me at the stake again?" She disappeared through the door to the science building, leaving Dan and Jasmine to exchange worried looks.

***

"Nice outfit!" Said Dan, genuinely admiring Claire in her black cat suit: the painted nose and whiskers, and the hair band with the pointy ears looked both cute and sinister in the dark street. "Love your tail!"

"Same old clown, I see!" was Claire's reply.

"You'd find it scary if you'd seen the film" said Dan, falling in step with her. "Look what I scrounged."

"Can't drink, can I? You should invest in a muppet costume next year!"

Simon's house was festooned with cotton wool cobwebs and plastic bats. There were pumpkin lanterns and gravestones on the lawn, and a sensor on the path that made the sound of a creaking castle door and a deep, evil laugh that sounded as if it were coming from the depths of a murky well. Claire and Dan pushed open the front door without ringing the bell, greeting the skeletons, vampires and zombies they met in the dimly lit hall. A creepy dirge of Gothic rock was playing at party volume as they moved further into the house. Simon was in the lounge, dressed as a very elaborate mummy, wrapped in grubby bandages and dusted with a layer of flour. His eyes had been blacked with face paint and were hardly visible through the holes in the bandages, and when he spoke, his mouth looked equally gruesome.

"Hey, you two, glad you could make it! Looking good, Claire! There's drinks in the kitchen; mum's made some fruit punch, but there's proper stuff too. Help yourselves."

"Thanks," said Dan. "Love the music, great atmosphere."

"Blair Witch soundtrack," shouted Simon, heading to the front door to scare some 3rd year trick-or-treaters.

"Fruit punch?" Dan suggested to Claire.

"Of course. I'm a good girl, remember!" she laughed, leading the way to the kitchen. More pumpkin lanterns illuminated the kitchen, where bats and vampires were talking in groups. There were cans of beer and cider, bottles of cheap wine, some bowls with crisps and pretzels, and a cauldron of fruit punch on the table next to some plastic cups and two empty vodka bottles the size of large hip flasks.

They filled their plastic goblets using the ladle, then both drained them down.

"Mmm, not bad," judged Claire, refilling her cup.

They moved through the ghouls and ghosts to the dining room, where Jasmine was playing spin the bottle.

"Claire, Dan, you made it! Come and join in! Guys, move back, make some space." The circle widened, and Claire and Dan sat down.

Over the canter of drums, Rob Zombie's unearthly voice crooned "Do it baby, do it baby".

The boy next to Claire span the bottle, and they all watched, nodding and swaying to the music, as it slowed to point at a girl in a classic witch's outfit.

"Third time! Upstairs!" Shouted a werewolf, and everybody joined in with cheers and grunts. The two got up and left the room, the boy revelling in the encouragement from the group.

> "Dead I am the dog,
> Hound of Hell you cry
> Devil on my back
> I can never die."

Sang Rob Zombie as guitars howled and whined eerily through the speakers.

Claire span the bottle, and it came to rest pointing at the gap where the witch had been, where now only a pumpkin lantern could be seen on the windowsill.

"Kiss the pumpkin!" Someone cried, then the whole circle was chanting "Kiss the pumpkin! Kiss the pumpkin!"

"Do it baby, do it baby," urged Rob Zombie.

Claire crawled like a cat towards the pumpkin as everyone whooped and jeered. She stood up, and lifted it off the sill, turning to face the room. Slowly and theatrically, she raised her grinning suitor up as she walked back to the middle of the circle, her face transformed by the flickering light. She stood gazing into the pumpkin's eyes at the flame dancing inside. The pumpkin gazed back at Nora Styles.

"Do it, baby," the flame whispered. "Do it."

The writers

Lois Elsden

Lois Elsden is passionate about writing; she was born and brought up in Cambridge, and having spent most of her adult life in Manchester, she now lives in a small Somerset village by the sea.

Lois writes full time and has published nineteen books, including two anthologies with other writers. She has written seven mystery novels, a guide to creative writing 'So You Want to Write', and three novels for reluctant readers.

Her Radwinter series of six genealogical mysteries follows Thomas Radwinter's commissions to explore family history. However, he finds himself unexpectedly embroiled in other cases, including kidnapping, abduction, attempted murder, secret sects and haunted hotels… oh and stalkers and serial killers. The next in the series, Winterdyke, will be published in late spring 2019 and is an old fashioned country house murder mystery!

Lois belongs to two writing collectives, 'Writers in Stone' and 'The Moving Dragon Writes'; she leads creative writing and family history writing groups, travels round the country to live music events, and watches the world go by in her local pub.

You can read Lois's blog on WordPress.

Elsa Heath

Elsa is 27 years old and her love of writing started at university where she studied English Language. She has always loved reading, especially books which transport her instantly to another world (needless to say, she's a big fan of Harry Potter!) When not working in local government or reading, she also likes going to the cinema and to concerts. Her short story is inspired by the fantasy novels from her childhood so she hopes you enjoy it.

Fenja Hill

Like many people, Fenja spent years believing she could write at least as well as some of the authors she read, if only she had the time. Meanwhile, she worked in jobs ranging from phlebotomy, van-driving and child-care to project management, consultancy and IT training. She says that her desire to keep changing jobs may have been because all she ever really wanted to do was write. She started three novels, but was always too tired or too busy to finish them. Finally, in 2017, she knew that she couldn't put it off any longer; if she was going to write, it had to be now.

She moved away from the city, to live in Weston-super-Mare, reduced her working hours and joined a creative writing group. One year later, she has published her first novel and is well on the way to completing her second. She is doing what she always wanted to do and is happier than she has ever been. Interestingly, the happier she is the darker the content of her writing. Make of that what you will.

What I did on my holidays: How to survive a disaster with nothing but a travel iron and a cuddly bunny

by Fenja Hill

How would you cope if you were washed up on an uninhabited island after your flight had crashed into the sea? Would you have a shelter built and a fire going by the end of the first day? Probably not. Real life is not like the books and films we have read and watched, which our heroine is about to find out.

Sue Johnson

Sue is the newest member of the group and the newest to writing. She has often been told by friends that she should put pen to paper and share her personal experience of mental ill health, and professional knowledge and experience from a career as a Social Worker with children and families. Now retired and a grandparent, she has decided to see if she can express some of her thoughts and emotions in poetry and prose. Two of her pieces appear here which, she says, without the encouragement and advice of 'Writer's in Stone' would never have emerged let alone metamorphosed into print!

Elizabeth Lawrence

Living most of her life by the sea in Cornwall, Elizabeth has always been moved and inspired by landscapes and nature, enjoying long walks, and combining two of her passions, poetry and photography, often writing descriptive verse to enhance photographic scenes.

Elizabeth developed an early love of classical literature and poetry, shared in great abundance at home with an encouraging mother and sisters. By her mid-teens, she had started writing poetry, taking inspiration from beauty and sadness around her – affected by the changing scenes and moods of nature, and greatly influenced by the pathetic fallacy style of the Brontës. She continued to write all her life, in the form of diaries, long letters and descriptive pieces, and was often asked to compose a poem or speech for weddings and funerals. Seeing people laugh and cry over her work, the turning point for Elizabeth was the realisation that she strikes a chord of empathy and has a voice worth hearing. Sensitive to literature all her life, the concept that others could be deeply affected by her work was a revelation and an impetus to continue, drawing on empathy, insight, and life experience. Her style of writing is mostly autobiographical, poetic prose with reflective thoughts and concepts, and along with the Writers in Stone, is experimenting with other styles and genres, and enjoying the experience, immensely!

Five years ago Elizabeth moved from Cornwall to Weston-super-Mare with her husband and daughter; enjoying the raw, natural beauty, ever-changing light and spectacular sunsets with great scope for photography. Discovering a book group and then its offshoot, Writers in Stone, she also found an outlet for her literary and creative needs, with stimulation and encouragement – a second home with likeminded people and a strong friendship group. In this exciting year, Elizabeth has also become a Bath Story Teller, writing and telling her own stories in the traditional way without notes, and launched her first open mic poetry reading. "From little acorns …."

Macaque

Macaque is essentially a frustrated artist, and has been writing poetry and stories since childhood, when he discovered that he could convey the emotions evoked in him by things he saw much better with a pen than with a brush. As a student, he was involved with various open mic and discussion groups, and whilst living in France, could be found most nights in bars discussing literature, philosophy and politics over red wine and absinthe. He wrote poems in French, and was delighted when he won second prize in a photography competition by submitting a poem written in black ink in the monochrome category. Later, as a post graduate student in Leicester, he was even more surprised to discover he had won the G.S. Fraser poetry prize, unaware that his tutor had entered one of his poems on his behalf.

In his younger days, Macaque would make booklets of his work by hand as gifts for friends, but his first collection **Palimpsest of Ghosts** is now available on Amazon. The collection deals with memories, and the events and encounters that create them, adding lines of sorrow or joy to our faces. Themes of love, loss, and observations of people and places are presented in a variety of poetic styles, all written with a visceral emotional voice. He is currently working on a second book of poetry, and a collection of short stories.

Macaque has lived in Somerset for the last five years, and has been regularly active in writing groups and open mic events in the region. Many of his recent poems have taken inspiration from the local scenery, not to mention the local cider. He spends much of his free time in the cafes and pubs around Weston-super-Mare, writing, rewriting, and making use of the free Wi-Fi. Rewriting and editing is the laborious process that, for Macaque, turns a flash of inspiration, an idea, a phrase, or a mental image, into a poem or story that will have an impact on the reader or listener, but more importantly, will meet his own exacting standards for his art.

Louise Pople

Louise has lived all her life in and around Weston-super-Mare. After taking early retirement from teaching, she embarked on getting fit through walking. The following year, she walked across England on the Coast to Coast path with a friend who has an interest in drama. To help pass the many hours of marching through the countryside, Louise contributed ideas to a pantomime Robin Hood, which was subsequently performed by Bleadon Players. On their return, inspired by the walk, Louise wrote a one act play "The Retirement Plan" which gained Highly Commended at The Somerset Fellowship of Drama Original Playwriting Competition and Festival, along with another play "What Would Caesar Do?" which gained a Commended at the same festival, and is due to be performed locally this year. Louise has continued to write One Act plays for festival competitions and was happy to be involved in the Writers in Stone writing group from its outset. "You can't help to be inspired by being surrounded by such talented creative people!" Louise is at present working on plays for the stage and radio.

Brenda Shrewsbury

Brenda has garnered experiences, events, ideas and snippets for as long as she can remember. One day she promised herself she would have a go at turning some of these "gems" into stories or one act plays. Early retirement arrived along with her first grandchild; retirement, what retirement? So the plan to explore creative writing was put on hold, then along came the chance to join Writers in Stone. What an amazing group of people who have supported and encouraged. She has co-written two pantomimes, both of which have been performed locally, and entered short story and One Act play competitions. Yet to be a winner, but she lives in hope!

Index of Pieces □

50 Words about Fear	Macaque	21
50 Words about Love	Macaque	24
A Definition of Excitement	Fenja Hill	11
An Idea of Heaven	Fenja Hill	100
Ballet Rehearsal, 1873	Macaque	17
Barriers	Elizabeth Lawrence	71
Beach Treasures	Elizabeth Lawrence	93
Best Friends Forever?	Fenja Hill	81
Bride and Groom	Elizabeth Lawrence	16
Cherry and Glory Pride	Lois Elsden	116
Coventry Road	Macaque	152
Dragon Story Time	Brenda Shrewsbury	110
Feel My Pain	Louise Pople	61
Haunting 101	Fenja Hill	145
If I Drift	Fenja Hill	95
Jetsam Coming Home	Jane Barron	89
Just a Trim	Louise Pople	22
Language Enrichment	Elizabeth Lawrence	84
Lifelines	Elizabeth Lawrence	27
Lucy Comes Home	Fenja Hill	57
Maud	Brenda Shrewsbury	64
Menu	Macaque	86
Mirror Images	Elizabeth Lawrence	45
Northern Roots	Elizabeth Lawrence	119
On Reflection	Brenda Shrewsbury	51
Pride	Jane Barron	115
Renewal	Elizabeth Lawrence	132
Rhythms of Life	Elizabeth Lawrence	104
Schrodinger's Chronometer	Macaque	106
Stone Love	Sue Johnson	131
The Bay	Louise Pople	32
The Bone-Yard	Macaque	41
The Mail-Order delivery	Elsa Heath	55
The Nutcracker	Macaque	133
The Proposal	Elizabeth Lawrence	23
The Real World of Daydreams	Elizabeth Lawrence	59
The Return	Elizabeth Lawrence	72
The Seventh Deadly Sin	Brenda Shrewsbury	125
The Silent Valley	Elizabeth Lawrence	149

The Sunfold	Macaque	31
The Three Mummers	Lois Elsden	145
The Wall	Louise Pople	73
This is the entrance...	Lois Elsden	37
Time-slip	Jane Barron	99
Two Haiku on the Theme of Pride	Sue Johnson	118
Uncle Pete	Elizabeth Lawrence	14
Webs we Weave	Jane Barron	139
Wind Chimes	Macaque	48
Yin and Yang	Elizabeth Lawrence	39

Index of writers

Jane Barron

Jetsam Coming Home	91
Pride	115
Time-Slip	99
Webs We Weave	139

Lois Elsden

Cherry and Glory Pride	116
This is the entrance…	37
The Three Mummers	145

Elsa Heath

The Mail-Order delivery	55

Fenja Hill

A Definition of Excitement	11
An Idea of Heaven	100
Best Friends Forever?	81
Haunting 101	145
If I Drift	95
Lucy Comes Home	57

Sue Johnson

Stone love	131
Two Haiku on the Theme of Pride	118

Elizabeth Lawrence

Barriers	71
Beach Treasures	93
Bride and Groom	16
Language Enrichment	84
Lifelines	27
Mirror Images	45
Northern Roots	119
Renewal	132
Rhythms of Life	104
The Proposal	23
The Real World of Daydreams	59
The Return	72
The Silent Valley	149
Uncle Pete	14
Yin and Yang	39

Macaque
50 Words about Fear   21
50 Words about Love   24
Ballet Rehearsal, 1873   17
Coventry Road   152
Menu   86
Schrodinger's Chronometer   106
The Bone-Yard   41
The Nutcracker   133
The Sunfold   31
Wind Chimes   48

Louise Pople
Feel My Pain   61
Just a trim   22
The Bay   32
The Wall   73

Brenda Shrewsbury
Dragon Story Time   110
Maud   64
On Reflection   51
The Seventh Deadly Sin   126

Printed in Poland
by Amazon Fulfillment
Poland Sp. z o.o., Wrocław

50682410R00096